The Old Rider

The Old Rider

J.S. Stroud

All rights reserved. No part of this book may be reproduced or transmitted in any form or by any means, electronic or mechanical, including photocopying, recording, or by any information storage and retrieval system, without permission in writing from the copyright owner.

This is a work of fiction. Names, characters, places and incidents either are the product of the author's imagination or are used fictitiously, and any resemblance to any actual persons, living or dead, events, or locales is entirely coincidental.

This book was printed in the United States of America.

Copyright © 2011 by J.S. Stroud

All rights reserved.

ISBN: 1-4610-7884-9
ISBN-13: 9781461078845

No one paid much attention to the rider on the stallion; he was nobody, just another drifter and if they looked at all the only thing they would have noticed was that was not wearing spurs. This was cattle country where men lived by the gun, the rope and the spur. It was strange to see a man without a pair of the star shaped tools attached to his boots, even the faded black hat had turned brown with age brought him no attention. There was a dark brown sweat stain along the wide brim of the hat that shaded the rider's eyes from the heat of the midday sun. From his head to his toes he spoke of being a worn out tired old drifter. He did not wear the bright colored bandana like the younger cowboys, in fact there was nothing around his neck, even the brace of twin colts looked old and used. Few looked up into the weather beaten face of the man but all eyes were on the stallion beneath him. This was an animal they had seen only in their dreams. Its eyes were like black coals of fire, the air from its nostrils seemed to form a haze that brought those eyes to life and every step it took spoke of power and strength. This animal had never run with the wild herds, it had led them! The scars on its chest and legs spoke of the battles it had been in to earn him the right to lead. Men and children alike stood stone still on the wooden side walk to watch them go by. Many of them had never seen an animal like this and few ever thought they would see one again. Tamer horses tied to the hitching rail shied away from the savage beast as they approached. The tracks in the soft dirt of the street showed that this was one horse that had never been shod. It carried no brand and was mastered by none. It was as savage at heart as it was in spirit. The Indians called it the black ghost or midnight phantom. It had been in their villages many times always at night and always to steal. The black stallion with the with the white chest and mane was well known in the villages, it came in like a ghost and the white mane and chest would flash in the night air as it attacked the stallions trying to guard their own herds. One or a dozen it made no difference, the battles were always the same, young strong horses went down under its hooves busted and bruised, it earned the name sudden death from these raids. Young warriors who had grown up on the stories told about the daring raids of the magnificent horse. It became a legend in its own time both feared and loved. Every child in the village dreamed of being the one to catch, ride and win the greatest horse alive and this was it!

The rider turned off the dirt street and rode into the stable, he noticed that the first two stalls were filled as he rode by but he was looking for the last stall, the one furthest from the rest of the horses. The cowboy's body leaned forward as his boot came over the saddle and his left hand held onto the saddle horn for balance as he slid to the ground below. The right hand hovered over the butt of the pistol at his side; something about the rider said he was more than he appeared to be. After removing the saddle, blanket and bridle he found a brush and begun to curry the animal, wiping the light froth from its mouth and body. He then poured some grain into the troth and closed the gate; this would do until his return. Pulling the brim of his hat down, he hid his face from the sun before leaving the stables. Men, women and children gathered on the sidewalk hoping to get another glimpse of the horse that had just mesmerized everyone who looked at it, was this really the horse, there couldn't be another one like him on the face of the earth!

No one ever noticed the rider as he walked by; this was the way of his life. There was a slight thumping sound beneath his boots as he walked to the Crooked Horn restaurant and bar. The rider had never been there before but it looked like a hundred other saloons with two painted windows in front and bat wing doors. It would be dark inside and most of the cowboys would step through those doors and stop, letting their eyes adjust to the cave like setting but not him, he leaned against the wall between the doors and the window briefly closing his eyes to let them adjust to the darkness before stepping through the swinging doors. The room was long and narrow, thirty feet wide and sixty feet long and more than a dozen tables were scattered about in a sloppy manner. A blond haired, blue eyed gorilla looking fellow with a scar running down his face stood polishing a shot glass behind the bar. Don't freeze up cowboy we don't bite, the voice came from one of the waitresses standing at a pot bellied stove sipping coffee. He walked to the nearest table and sat down. The young waitress spoke again, he's all yours mom. The older waitress liked annoyed and came back with "I told you not to call me that!" Why is it that every cowboy in the country call's me mom? Well, Marilyn, Sheila answered, it could be because you've been twenty nine longer than most of us can count! Marilyn picked the tally book up off the corner of the bar and headed for the table. What will it be Ace, a grin of mischief was on her face. What's edible and what's any good the man asked, as a second thought after catching a whiff the aroma coming from the kitchen. It depends on the cook, whether she is reading, sleeping or eating. If you want to order the biscuits they're gonna be burned, if you order the beans they're gonna be burned and if you order the gravy it's gonna be lumpy and burned, Marilyn laughed, trying to get a smile out of the man. The cook will have one of her children kill a chicken if you like. The younger waitress spoke up again, yeah, and you better grab the chicken when it hits the table cause its tough enough to fly off ten minutes after its cooked! Marilyn gave the younger waitress a look of disdain, shut up Sheila, you couldn't boil water in a volcano and you know it. Turning back to the man Marilyn asked again, "what will it be Ace?" I guess its biscuits and beans, he said. Marilyn smiled at the man she called Ace and said "it's your funeral" and with that she turned and walked away. Joe leaned back in his chair and watched her leave. Maybe this town was not so bad after all.

Marilyn looked over at the bartender and said "hey, Paul, you better bring this gent a cup of that black crap you call coffee, he's gonna need it to choke down one of Eloise's biscuits." Paul picked up a cup and began to pour the piping hot beverage, "Ain't nothing gonna help them biscuits, he muttered under his breath as he set it on the table in front of Joe. Joe picked up the cup of coffee with a grimace, in his opinion it needed three things, sugar, cream and a burial. It was probably the worst coffee he had ever tasted. After a few sips he put the cup down and looked around the room, there was not much to it; a couple of broken down cowboys stood at the bar with their boots hooked over the rail and their spurs dragging the floor. At one table half a dozen men sat playing poker and over in a corner sipping coffee was a dark skinned man wearing black clothing with a tied down revolver. Marilyn came back with a large bowl of beans with several hard tack biscuits on top. "Ace if I was you, I would soak them biscuits in the beans before I tried eating them and with that she sat down in the chair across the table from Joe. He could not take it anymore, "alright lady my name is", "my name is Marilyn, she cut in", alright Marilyn, why do you keep calling me Ace? Why that's simple Marilyn answered, your eyes are too narrow, your smile never reaches your eyes and no matter what you're doing, one of your hands never strays far from the pistols at you side. It just makes me think you're the better half of the dead man's hand. Joe began to smile, it was more of a lopsided grin, his hand still hung at his side close to the worn out 44 revolver. He was paying too much attention to Marilyn when the bat wing doors flew open banging both side of the wall as a young cowboy came into the room. He was not walking and he was not running, he was stumbling. Two other cowboys came in behind him laughing and joking. "Hey Mike, can't you stand up", laughed the largest of the three. Mike turned towards the speaker, "not with you pushing me", he yelled, doubling up his fists and starting towards the speaker. "Now Mike, you know what happened the last time you tangled with Roy." "Bobby you stay out of it or you will be the next one I slug," Bobby began to laugh, "Now Mike; you know what happened the last time you tried that too. Mike began to settle down. Joe started to relax, without thinking he had slumped back in the chair the revolver in the cross draw holster was pulled half way out and his thumb was starting to pull the hammer as he realized they were just a couple of drunken cowboys out for some fun. Marilyn sat across the table white faced and in shock but within seconds she found her voice, "Ace" she said, "I like them boys and if you kill any one of them you better shoot me too because if you don't I'm gonna put a hole in your back the sheriff will be able to ride a horse through!" With that she stood up and left. The cowboy called Roy, slapped Bobby in the back of the head and Bobby grabbed Roy's arm and slung him in a half circle smacking him face first into the wall next to the bat wing doors. Roy was half stunned as Mike and Bobby both grabbed his boots and flipped him to the floor and dragged him to the bar, seeing Marilyn the combat stopped and Bobby and Mike both came out with "hi mom" at the same time. Roy tried to get into a sitting position, "hi mom" came out of the giant grin on his face. Marilyn was not impressed and she cut loose with both barrels, "don't call me mom!" if I was your mother I'd have drowned all three of you, Mike began to laugh, "now mom, you know we all can swim. Bobby piped up with you betcha! Marilyn started to fume, "I meant at birth" she said. It was Roy's turn to laugh. "Heck" he said, "when do you think we learned to swim?" She could not win a battle of wits with the smart-alecky kids, walking to the bar she drew out a twelve inch iron skillet, Mike, Roy and Bobby all drew back in mock fear, "Oh no!" Bobby cried, she is going to hit me with a skillet! All three of them laughed at the threat, they had Marilyn now and they knew it! "That thing is loaded" one of them cried "it's full of Eloise's beans!" all three were rolling with laughter. They were on a roll. Eloise was fifty-four years old, tough and grizzled, the truth was Eloise was actually a good cook but for the last two weeks she had been training her daughter Terry. Terry could rope, shoot and ride but when it came to cooking people said she would butcher a cow thinking it was a hog. Eloise was part owner and Marilyn felt she had to be loyal to her partner. She could pester and pick at the cook but she did not want anyone else to. Besides bad mouthing the food was not going to help the business. Mike may have been the youngest but he had the quickest eye and he saw one more chance to pester Marilyn, "hey mister," he turned his attention to the man sitting at the table, "soaking them cast iron plow disks in beans ain't gonna help none. Last week I tried nailing one to a fence post and all I did was bend some good nails." Bobby began to laugh, "Shucks" he said, "that ain't nothing, why only this morning I threw one in the air for target practice and when I shot the darn thing, the ricochet nearly took my head off. Roy could see the banter was making Marilyn upset and moved to the bar. "Hey, unck set up two whiskies for me and Bobby and give the boy here a cup of coffee," pointing in the direction of Mike. "I ain't your uncle," Paul said, with a snarl, "you keep calling me that and one day I'm gonna hit you so hard your momma's gonna cry." "Go ahead, hit him, see if I care, besides, he's so ugly his momma moved to Ireland just to get away from him." Roy turned red and started towards the younger man with his fists doubled. "You keep popping off and I'm the one who is going to be doing the slugging!" A smarter man might have shut up but Mike did not care, he liked antagonizing the bigger man. "Oh, I'm sorry," he said "after all it's your daddy that's so ugly, his twin is the back side of a mule." Mike never saw the fist as it hit him! He went backwards, tripping over a chair and landing flat on his back. His head was still ringing as Roy approached, "maybe I pushed it to far this time" he thought as Roy grabbed his shirt and jerked him to his feet. Mike shook his head trying to clear the cobwebs and realized another blow was coming, it found its mark on the left side of his head. Lights flashed and the roar of a waterfall exploded as the blow landed. Through a hazy fog Mike saw the left fist coming, the blow was meant to take his head off but this time he was ready and jerked back, the knuckles of Roy's hand sliced through the air spinning his body around. Roy was off balance as Mike threw a right of his own, it was a lucky punch and landed hard behind Roy's left ear, now Mike was the one moving forward, his left hand swung in a circle trying to force the fight. Roy leaned forward lifted his right foot and drove it backwards with all the strength he could muster. The heel of the western riding boot sank deep into the flesh below Mike's rib cage stopping him in his tracks. For a second Mike thought he was going t be sick, the air was forced from his lungs as pain shot through his entire body. Mike stumbled back trying to catch his breath. He had been hit before but nothing like this, the fight was forgotten and all he wanted to do was get one lousy breath of air. Roy was turning to pursue the fight as the roar of a small cannon was heard in the room, both men looked towards the bar, Paul stood there with a double barreled shot gun in his hands. Both men knew that Paul had fired a paper wad into the ceiling. One barrel of the weapon was still smoking, the other remained loaded. Alright, that's enough! You two yahoos ain't gonna tear this place apart again he said. Eloise and Marilyn came running from the kitchen at the sound of the blast. "Paul put that down" she screamed. "But mom," Paul stated "I was just trying to break them up." "I don't care what you were trying to do, she yelled, "you don't need a shotgun to do it!" Joe sat at the table watching the family feud, a crooked smile on his face. Marilyn turned on the boys, "you three pack it up and get out of here!" Bobby spoke up, "it wasn't me!" Marilyn's eyes went fire red, "Go home and sleep it off before I have the sheriff in here!" "Like heck, I am," Mike said, "I'm going to Nita's." "Hey unck, give me a bottle of tequila will ya." Paul slid the bottle across the bar ignoring the familiar remark of the younger man.

As Bobby, Roy and Mike started for the door; Marilyn walked across the room and set down across the table from Joe. "They're just wild kids," she said making excuses for their behavior. Joe looked into her soft brown eyes, "dang" he thought, "why am I still setting here, I should be a hundred miles down the road!" Marilyn looked back into the hard cold eyes of the man in front of her. She had missed the brief look softness that had flash across his mind before he managed to hide it. A shiver went through her very soul, here sat a man as cold and vicious as any she had ever met, yet she felt drawn to him, there was something about him . . .

As the boys exited the bar one of the card players stood up. If they come back in here again I'm gonna put a bullet in them. The man speaking was a tall man wearing the dress of a gambler, with a tied down short barreled revolver at his side. He may have been a gambler but the quick draw gun rig left no doubt he knew how to use it. Marilyn stood up, "you'll leave them alone," she said with venom in her voice. The gambler spoke again, "you woman, forget that I am part owner in this place and I'll blow the hell out of them!" Joe could not believe what he was doing, before he knew it he was sliding out of the chair, his right hand hung over the handle of the pistol on his left side, just inches from the cross draw holster. "Mister, you got three seconds to draw or die." Joe could not care less about the boys, he was thinking of the soft brown eyes of the waitress. Marilyn began to yell for William to sit down. She only called him William when he was upset; "sure," he said reaching for the chair behind him with both hands. Then with the sped of a snake he drew. His thumb cocked the hammer of the revolver as it came up, the left hand came forward ready to fan the pistol after the first shot. William knew he was fast and accurate and that the little trick gave him an added advantage and he was sure no man alive could match his speed. As the pistol in his hand began to raise Williams face took on a look of terror. Joe's right hand flashed, the pistol was cocked and flames erupted out of the barrel even before William's pistol had a chance to clear leather. The slam of the bullet told him that he had been struck in the chest. The barrel of the pistol spit fire twice more, both times he felt the impact of the pieces of lead as they drove deep into his flesh. Staggering back he set in the very chair he had been reaching for. William looked down, it was strange, his pistol was back in its holster and three holes had been blown through the front of his shirt. William managed a weak smile and said "I think I'm gonna take a nap," with that he slumped face first to the hard wood floor below. Joe stood in the gun fighter's stance facing the men at the table. If they so much as flinched he was gonna blow their heads off. Marilyn started to step between Joe and the men at the table; she had seen enough of the killing. Joe turned facing her; the look of a cold blooded killer stopped her in her tracks. She had seen men killed before but nothing like this. Joe glanced back at the table, no one moved. William may have been their friend but no one wants to die for a dead man. Joe's eyes began to soften; the hard lines of his face took on the look of a nobody. Marilyn began to shiver, she knew she stood before a chameleon, a man capable of changing his looks at will and the most dangerous man she had ever met. Joe saw the fear in her eyes and slid the pistol back into the holster; he had not meant to terrify the woman. With the most charming smile he could muster Joe said, "Well you've got one less partner." Marilyn thought she was going to be sick. Joe sat back down at the table and took a drink of the strong coffee. "Might as well wait for the marshal," he said, one hand still resting over the butt of his pistol.

 Johnny Vasquez walked up to the body; he was the man in the black suit hidden in the corner. He did not want people to know who he was or why he was here but this was something he had to see. Looking down he counted a dozen holes in the back of William's shirt! This was something he had heard of but had never seen before but he knew what had happened, the nobody gunman, the one the waitress called "Ace", carried two pistols, one loaded with solid shells, the other carried shells with deep X's cut into the end of the bullets. The deep cuts in these shells would split apart on impact, going off in different parts of the body. William was proof of the damage they could do; his back looked like someone had used a shotgun up close. Johnny Vasquez was a professional gunman. He carried nine notches on his guns and he had been paid five hundred dollars to add three more. Vasquez looked at 'Ace' and decided he was not getting paid enough! Johnny turned and headed for the door as the marshal and two deputies pushed the bat wing doors open, pistols in their hands. Vasquez stood still, the slightest move and he had no doubt he would be the next to die. Three forty-four caliber pistols were pointed at his guts. Slowly he began to raise his hands. After they were shoulder high he spoke for the first time. "Was not me," he said. Sweat was beginning to appear on his upper lip and his hands were shaking slightly. This had never happened to him before and he did not like this feeling at all! He was thinking of the five hundred dollars in his pocket, the bottle of tequila in his saddle bags and the woman in Sonora. If he lived to make it to the door he was heading south. "Who was it then?" the larger of the three star packers asked. "The gunman," he stated quietly and slowly started for the door. Vasquez had not made two steps before he felt the barrel of a pistol being shoved into his back. "What gunman?" Vasquez turned to see Roger,(most folks called him Rog) the youngest of the deputies holding a cocked revolver. "Marshal, tell your deputy to put that thing away before he shoots the wrong man. "Vasquez, you tell us what gunman or I'll have him shoot you myself!" The thought that the marshal and the deputy's knew who he was upset him. Somebody must have warned them about him coming into town. Vasquez had noticed 'Ace' when he came into the saloon and thought like most people that he was a nobody, then watched as he transformed into a deadly gunman and then just as quickly turned back into the role of a invisible drifter! "He's the only one wearing two guns." The marshal was tired of the short answers and the fast guns attitude. "You better pack up and leave before I find something to jail you for." As the marshal walked past him into the saloon Vasquez turned cold, he knew he could beat the marshal in a gun fight but he had a hunch he better kill him with the first bullet or he was gonna catch lead himself. "Marshal, you could not pay me enough to stay in this town!" He walk out the door, swung his leg up over his horse and headed south, back to Sonora, the senoritas and the tequila, glad to be alive!

After one glance at the gambler called 'Wild Bill', Jim and the two deputies turned to the lone man setting at the table. He did not look like much and not the kind of man that could have taken Bill in a gunfight, still they weren't taking any chances, and all three held their weapons pointed at the man's chest. Joe leaned back; a hard cold look of molten steel came into his eyes. The marshal began to tighten his grip on the trigger, as he noticed the intense look coming from the stranger sitting before him, then just as quickly the man's eyes began to soften and his body relaxed. Joe stood up and with both hands in the air and then slowly lowered one hand and began to unbuckle the gun belt from around his waist. Schon, the second deputy who had entered with the Marshal and Rog, reached over and took the belt with his left hand while his right hand still held the pistol pointed at the man's chest, he was taking no chances. The two deputies walked Joe to the jail as the Marshal stayed behind to question the witnesses. It looked like a clear case of self defense; William had been the one to draw first. The deputies were drinking day old coffee as Jim entered the office. He walked to his desk and set down. Joe's pistols were hanging on the rack behind him. Schon walked over took their guns from their holsters and handed them to the Marshal. Johnny Vasquez had been right, the first weapon was a standard forty-four with a six inch barrel and solid lead bullets but the second pistol had been altered, the six inch barrel was cut down to five. The three remaining shells had deep X's cut in them, even the trigger was wired back. Everything about this set-up spoke of up close killing. Jim looked at the man behind the bars. He had never seen a man who could look as innocent and be so deadly at the same time. Jim emptied the gun cylinders and locked the weapons in his desk then he shoved the discarded shells into the empty loops of the gunman's belt. There was a rumor around town that the Rocking "R" was hiring gunmen. If it was true this man could be one of the best. There was no since worrying about it tonight, his wife, Sherlene, was waiting for him and supper would be ready when he got home. Jim pulled his slicker off the rack, pitched the cell keys to Schon and said you boys are in charge, I'm going home. "What are we gonna do about him?"

Schon asked, looking at the man lying on the bunk in his cell. "Get some sleep, the circuit Judge will be here in a few days and he can figure out what to do with him. Between now and then don't get too close to the bars."

It had been a long day. Joe laid back and went right to sleep, dreaming of brown eyes. "Wake up cowboy," Joe's eyes flew open at the sound. His right hand sprang for the pistol at his left side grabbing only air. Marilyn was entering the cell with a tray in one hand and a cup in the other. The smell of biscuits and gravy filled the room. Joe sat up as she handed him the tray, Marilyn took a sip of the strong black coffee from the cup and sat on the bunk next to Joe. "Why did you do it?" Joe liked kind of puzzled, "do what?" he asked. "Bill could have killed you," she said. Joe took on a sheepish grin, "Bill could not beat me in my sleep!" For a split second Marilyn was taken aback by the statement, and then she remembered the speed of his hand reaching for the missing revolver as he awoke. She decided then and there that Bill had been a dead man the second he had reached for the chair! Joe took the cup from Marilyn's hand and started to drink the hot beverage, "what about my horse?" he asked. Otis will take care of him, I'll see to that. "If you can manage it I would rather take care of him myself. Marilyn nodded, "I'll see what I can do." "While you're at it can you find out what they're holding me for?" "I already know that," she stated, "The Marshal rode out to the Rocking "R" to see if they hired you. "What's the Rocking "R" and why would they hire me?" "The Rocking 'R' is the biggest ranch in the country and growing." "To make sure nobody stops that growth, their bringing in gunmen form down south. Joe's eyes became hard and cold again, "and he went to see if I was for hire, right?" Marilyn did not know what to do or say, she had seen what he could do with a pistol, what did she think he was a saint or a store keeper? Marilyn picked up the tray and asked if he wanted more coffee, after a curt no she signaled the deputy to unlock the door. "Rog is there any chance you can let him out long enough to tend his horse," she asked as she crossed the room. The young deputy shook his head, "Marshal will be back after while, and we'll let him decide." Marilyn could not make up her own mind, she was doing things she had never done before. Sure the deputies ate at the restaurant but she had never delivered a meal before, not even for the three young cowboys and she would never have gone into a cell with a gunman but 'Ace' was different, he had a soft side, almost loveable, she though. Marilyn shook her head what was she thinking, how could anyone love a hired gun?

Joe watched the brown eyed waitress exit the cell. Life is strange he thought, six months ago he had sold his ranch and a hundred head of cattle, he was headed for the California gold fields. At that time he wanted nothing more than to strike it rich. He was tired of Oklahoma and the rock infested ground and in his opinion it was good for nothing but scrub brush, cattle and ticks. After buying a second pistol, a pack horse and a pick he had saddled up and headed west. Every night he dreamed of the saddle bags of gold he was going to find, the large ranch and fancy home he was going to buy with the gold and become master of. He dreamed of ocean voyages, great adventures and beautiful women. Then purely by accident he stumbled across a herd of wild horses. At the front of the herd was the black. Dreams of gold, big ranches and ocean voyages were forgotten. He had never wanted anything in his life more that he wanted the massive horses that lead the pack. Joe leaned back in his cell. All of his life he had been a loner, needing or wanting no one, a man alone. Joe continued to watch Marilyn as she left the office, the life of a lonely man came crashing down around him, the memories of a thousand campfires seemed to pull at him like chains, even the thought of the black could not break the feeling of despair. At that moment Joe wanted nothing more than to feel the warm arms of the brown eyed waitress around him, to look into her eyes and see the kind of love he had never known. The kind of love he had never dreamed possible.

Rog was locking the cell as a tall lanky cowboy came walking in. The Marshal was right behind him with the barrel of his pistol to the man's back. "Open the cell door" the Marshal commanded and as the deputy started to open the cell he had just locked the Marshal said, "the other cell, there's no use putting these two together." The Marshal had called the kid, K,C., and he was probably around twenty-one or two. He was what the ladies would call a good looking man. "What's going on Marshal?" Rog asked. It was hard to believe that they had two prisoners at one time and it wasn't even Saturday! "Rustler," was the reply and Roger seemed shocked by the news. "Him?" he said not trying to cover the surprise in his voice. "Him," said the Marshal in a cold flat voice. "Been stealing cattle over at the Malloy place." K.C. cut in with, "I ain't been stealing nothing!" "Seems he's been courting the old man's daughter and every time he comes around the old man ends up with better than half a dozen of his prim cattle missing, he is under the impression the young un is behind the thief's." "That's better," K.C. said but like I said I ain't stole nothing!" Rog locked the door behind him as K.C. headed for the bunk. "Hey, when am I getting out of here," he yelled, looking as if he had the world at his finger tips. Joe rolled over to get a better look at the cattle thief. The kid wore a pair of high topped hand tooled western riding boots, a flashy red shirt with silver buttons. The pistol on the Marshals desk had come out of a quick draw holster with a large silver star attached. Everything the kid wore spoke of money. K.C. looked annoyed as Joe rolled back over. "What are you looking at?" K.C. spat at him. Joe pulled his hat over his face and said "a hanged man." The young man went into a rage and threw the metal drinking cup at the bars of the cell. "When am I getting out of here?" he screamed. "That's up to the judge," the Marshal said as he was hanging the kid's gun belt on the rack, "Now settle down." "Well when is that?" he demanded. "In a week maybe two, depends on when he gets here," the Marshal answered. Joe sat up, "I can't leave my horse in a stall for the next two weeks." "Rog will feed him and put him in the corral until the hearing." "That black will kick his head in if he goes in that stall," Joe warned him. Rog looked at the Marshal, "Jim," he said, I've seen that monster and he's right, I ain't going in that stall!" Jim could not believe a horse had put fear into his deputy, "fine put a gun in his back and let him out of the cell. He can take care of his own dang horse!" Jim said as he left the office. Joe set up in his cell as Rog pitched him the keys that was all he wanted in the first place; Joe walked out of the Marshal's office with the pistol in his back. "You try anything and it will be the last thing you ever do," Rog warned him. The sound of the men's boots resounded on the wooden sidewalk as they headed for the town stable. "What are you gonna do with that?" the voice came from behind the deputy as they passed the Crooked Horn restaurant.

Rog fought back the urge to run; he had never fought a woman before and did not know if he could, especially this woman. Marilyn stood ready to attack. Fists doubled and eyes aflame. "Marshal's orders," he yelled trying to bring the woman to her senses. She screamed back, "you need a gun in his back to walk down the street?" the brown eyes had turned red with fury; every fiber in her was ready to explode. Rog did not know what to do, he had never been in this position before, "Jim said to keep a gun on him he explained." "It was self defense," she screamed, "What you think he is going to do kill you and run off. What good would that do? Every lawman in the country would be hunting him. He would become a wanted criminal for nothing." Rog slid the weapon into the holster, "fine," he said, "If he escapes you can tell that to your brother!" Marilyn stomped off still in a rage, "you can bet I'll take this up with my brother!" she said slinging the bat wing doors open so hard they banged into both walls. Joe look hard at the young deputy almost in shock, "she's the marshal's sister?" he asked. "Not really," the young man answered. "Jim is married to her sister Sherlene but they act like their blood kin. "Now let's go take care of that horse of yours before someone else decides to take my head off." The blacks ears picked up as Joe and the deputy walked into the barn. Rog stood back as Joe patted the blacks shoulder and neck. Joe talked softly to it trying to calm the animal as he slipped a sort rope over the horses head and opened the stall gate. Instantly the animal pulled back almost dragging Joe over the top rail as the gate was opened. It was a battle of wills and strength as the horse tried to break free. The animal pulled again and Joe was pulled over the railing still hanging onto the rope even as he was slammed to the ground. The black reared up and the action pulled Joe to his feet. Rog was beginning to think he was going to have to shoot the animal to save the man's life. As Rog reached for the pistol at his side, Joe ran to one side and grabbed hold of the white mane and kicked one leg up and latched on. The animal was rearing up again as Joe wrapped both arms around its neck. The horse half hopped and landed on its front feet slamming Joe's face into its neck. Joe lifted his leg as the horse spun and rammed its side into the nearest stall trying to drive the rider off. Joe muttered through gritted teeth, "open the gate." Rog swung the gate open and stepped out of the way as horse and rider bolted through. Joe slid to the ground and lay flat as the black spun his hind quarters and kicked out at the rider, the hoof missing his head by inches. Joe sat in the dirt with blood running from his mouth and nose, watching the horse run as Rog came over to help him up. "I don't think he liked the stall," Joe said as he got to his feet. "Neither do I," said the young deputy, "We'll stop by the Crooked Horn and get you cleaned up, providing you don't put the blame on me for you bleeding!" "Agreed," Joe said as he walked to the stall and picked up his saddle bag. Do you mind, my rifle is in the corner, it was the safest place I could think of when I came into town?" Rog picked up the rifle and they started for the Crooked Horn. Joe could not help but see the smile on the deputy's face. "What's so funny," he asked. "Oh, nothing, I was just thinking, one more ride like that and the judge won't have to hang you, that horse will kill you for him."

The Marshal, Marilyn, deputy Schon and a beautiful, brown haired woman with piercing hazel eyes sat at a table drinking coffee as Joe and Rog entered the restaurant. "Why ain't you got a gun on him," Jim asked. "Since you don't know what you're doing," Marilyn snapped. Jim looked at her, "Who put you in charge of the prisoners?" His annoyance was starting to show, as a red flush crept up his neck and the vein in his temple began to pulsate. "I did," she answered, "the minute you became an idiot!" Jim settled back in his chair with a puzzled look on his face, she's in love he thought. Marilyn walked over to the pot bellied stove took a pan down from the hook and filled it half full of water, "Sit down Ace" she said. "Joe walked over pulled out a chair and sat down. "How did this happen" she asked dipping a cloth into the warming pot of water. "Rog did it," Joe answered half laughing to himself. Marilyn spun on the deputy and Rog threw both hands in the air, "he's lying," he said as Marilyn took a step towards him. This time Joe broke out in laughter. This was a new sensation to him. He couldn't remember the last time he had laughed and it felt good. He hadn't had much to laugh about in his life. Even now he was a prisoner in this town and yet he felt comfortable with these people. "Maybe I'm just getting soft in my old age," he thought to himself, "Yeah, soft in the head."

Jim looked over at the dark hair woman, "Honey I think someone is in love!" It seemed Jim had a funny side to him or was he just trying to get even with Marilyn for telling him how to do his job? These thoughts were running through Joe's head when Sherlene, Jim wife, said, "that could never happen to my sister, she's the level headed one, she could never fall in love, just ask momma." Schon could not help it, the deputy busted out laughing. Jim and Sherlene joined in. Marilyn could hardly contain her anger; she threw the wet rag at the officer and stormed out of the room. Rog saw that it was safe and joined the others at the table. "Come on cowboy, let's get you back to your cell," he said as the laughter died down. Rog locked the cell door behind Joe, sat down at the Marshal's desk, spun the chair around and put his boots through the bars of the cell. "You sure like living on the edge cowboy,' he said. "How do you figure," Joe asked. "Well, you ride into town on a horse that's liable to kill you, get into a gun fight with one of the meanest men in town, and then you pick the marshal's sister for a girlfriend. I'd say you like living dangerously! Joe leaned back in his cell, he never thought of having a girlfriend before. Early the next morning as the other men in the jail slept Joe got up stretched his arms and legs for a few minutes, did some pull ups from the bars of his cell and then went into the gun fighters crouch and practiced his draw, first one hand then the other, grabbing imaginary weapons. He lived by the speed of his hands and the power of his arms, having a girlfriend was not going to stop a life time of habits. Joe forced his hands to remain by his side as he heard the cell door open. The smell of strong coffee filled the room as Marilyn entered the office. She carried a tray filled with pancakes smothered in butter and covered with homemade syrup; the smell of the food woke the man in the other cell. "Hey, where's mine," K.C. asked as he came to his feet. "I'll get yours later," Schon answered. "I want mine delivered by a pretty girl," K.C. complained. "I've been up with drunks all night," Schon growled, "You keep complaining and you won't get any!" "I liked the other guard better!" K.C. said as he went back to his bunk

Joe dug into the food, as Marilyn set down beside him she picked up his cup of coffee and began to take a sip, "what are your plans when you get out of here," she asked. "Don't really know," he answered. "I was headed to the California gold fields." Marilyn look puzzled, "what changed you mind," she asked. Joe didn't know what to say; he was not used to being around women and did not know how to confess his love. "I guess you could say the black did," he answered afraid to show his true feelings. Marilyn picked up the tray feeling a little hurt, not sure if he felt the same way about her as she felt about him. After the hearing would he ride off never to be seen again? Would she always remember the sad haunted eyes of the man in the cell? Could she ever forget the way he looked at her? Marilyn fought back the tears as she made her way to the Crooked Horn. Schon looked up from the Marshal's desk to see a young woman enter the office. She was around seventeen with a beautiful smile. "Can I help you?" he asked. "I'm here to see K.C.," she answered. "Sorry, you'll have to wait for the Marshal," Schon told her. Nicole turned on the charm, "I can't, pas coming and there's gonna be trouble," she explained. "Please just let me talk to K.C." She was a lovely young lady with long brown hair, big blue eyes and a smile that would soften a heart made of stone and Schon fell for that charm. "Fine but only for a few minutes, if the Marshal finds out it will be my hide," he exclaimed, not really afraid of Jim. Nicole flashed him a big smile and headed for the cell. "Can we have some privacy," she asked. Schon was a little perturbed but he stepped out of the office and onto the wooden sidewalk, "great you're going to get me fired," he complained taking the keys with him. K.C. jumped up from the rod iron bed and met Nicole at the bars of the cell. "Honey," he whispered "I've got half a hundred head of prim cattle hidden in a corral on the north side of your old man's ranch. Their down in a draw with a small creek in it and I want you to ride up there and let them go. They will drift back to the old man's place and they will have to let me go!" "Why don't we just keep the cattle," she said. K.C. began to worry, "because your old man will have me hung," he explained. Nicole turned on the charm again, "no he won't," she said "I told him I was pregnant." K.C.'s jaw looked like it was going to hit the floor. "That ain't possible," he nearly shouted. Nicole's smile turned bitter sweet, "tell daddy that and he will hang you himself!" Nicole had the upper hand on both men and she knew it! Schon opened the front door and stood there, "sorry kids, Marshal's on the way, you better go." Nicole was all honey and smiles swinging her hips as she turned and walked out of the room.

That afternoon Don Malloy and half a dozen of his men rode into town. Swinging down from their mounts they flipped the reins over the hitching post and walked into the bar section of the Crooked Horn, "my little girl's getting married," he said as the men lined up for the free drinks "and if she don't get married?" one of the men asked, "then we're gonna have us a hanging!" was the replay from the speaker. Every man there knew he was speaking the truth. Don Malloy may have been a lot of things but he was as good as his word and K.C. Jones was in big trouble! Don Malloy started out of the room, "you two follow me, and the rest of you stay here and get drunk." No one was going to argue about the free drinks and lined up at the bar and none of them were going to argue with the man who believed his daughter had been violated. Schon jumped to his feet as the men entered the office, every fiber of his being knew something was about to explode. Don Malloy stood glaring at the deputy. "I want to see that no good cattle rustler!" he said. By the look of pent up rage on the weather beaten face, Schon knew this was not about cattle and things were about to get out of hand. The deputy hated to draw on another man but he had no choice, the pistol leapt into his hand and was pointed at the stomach of the older man. "Mr. Malloy, I don't want to have to kill you he said so please drop your weapon." Malloy was tempted to force the deputy's hand but the better part of common sense stilled his hand. "Fine," he said as he unbuckled the gun belt and threw it on the Marshal's desk. "I still want to see the cattle thief!" Schon shook his head, "not with your men standing behind me your not!" Malloy did not like the play but he turned to his men, "you boys head back to the Crooked Horn, I'll meet you there after I'm done here." He was not a patient man, "alright their gone, he said; now I want to see this thief face to face." "Fine," Schon said, just keep your hands outside of the cell. K.C. lay back on the bunk of his cell and watched the big man approach. K.C. broke the silence, "I didn't steal nothin," he stated flatly. Don Malloy exploded, "we ain't talking about cattle and you know it! You got two words to say, 'I do' or you can die. Cause if you don't I'll see you hanged!" "You can't hang a man for nothing,

K.C. complained. The eyes of the old man burned with a fury K.C. had never seen before. "I found twenty head of my cattle carrying a K.C. brand in my south pasture." K.C. could not believe what he was hearing, "that's impossible," he said starting to feel nervous for the first time. "You planted them!" "Prove it," the old man said. "Like I said, you are gonna set in this cell until the justice of the piece gets here and then your gonna say I do or your gonna hang." With that Malloy left the jail and headed for the Crooked Horn. After the soon to be father-in-law departed Joe turned to look at the rustler. "Crap, I thought I had problems," he said as he rolled over, pulled his hat over his head and went to sleep. There was nothing to do in the small confines of a jail cell and Joe was getting used to the short cat naps. Schon rattled the cage door and Joe awoke. "Hey, you play checkers?" he asked. "Sure do," Joe answered. Schon unstrapped his gun belt laid it on the desk, pitched the cell keys on top and slid a card table against the bars of the cell. "What about me," K.C. whined. "Three can't play at the same time." Schon opened one of the drawers on the marshal's desk, "here," he said pitching a pack of cards into the cell with the rustler. The Marshal took them from a whisky drummer last month, their marked so try not to cheat yourself!" K.C. began to spread the cards out in a pyramid fashion for a game of solitaire as Joe set up the checker board. "Where you from," Schon asked as Joe jumped two of his men. Joe stopped and studied the face of the deputy to see if he really wanted to know or to see if he was just doing his job, trying to figure the man out. After a few seconds he decided the deputy really wanted to know. "Oklahoma," he said "the land of rocks snakes and weeds." "That's what I've heard," Schon said, "but is it really that bad?" "You can bet your saddle on it! My place had more rocks than cattle and more snakes than weeds and there were plenty of both, heck, how do you think I got so good with a pistol? I spent half of my day popping the heads off them big old velvet tailed rattlers." "Well what about the sawed off pistol with no sights and the knife cut shells?" he asked. Joe shook his head, "it's plain to see you've never been to Oklahoma!" "No," Schon answered, "Why?" "You ain't never seen a razor back hog, then have you?' "Not that I can recall." "If you did you would not forget it. They are a long skinny animal with a hump back and razor like tusks. They run in packs and can take a man's horse out from under him in about three seconds. Fellow, you don't want to be on the ground with a pack of them around cause they will kill you in heart beat and what they kill they eat, be it man, horse or dog!" "That still don't explain the sawed off pistol or the X cut shells?" Schon stated. "Sure it does, those things come out of the brush nearly at you feet and they come at a run, you gotta get your gun out quick. You don't want to have a pistol stick in the holster or hang up on a sight. As far as the cut shells, I found one bullet won't always stop the darn things but a shell ripping apart on impact will stop a hog in its tracks." " But at thirty feet those shells are almost worthless," the deputy said, "you could not hit the broad side of a barn with them, besides that they could spread out in the barrel and blow your hand off if not your head!" "Yep," Joe admitted, "that could happen but I spent a lot of time and practice perfecting that cut. Anymore and it could blow up in the barrel and any less and it won't spread." "You can keep those shells," Schon said, "I ain't about to fire them." "To each his own," Joe stated. "Hey, I can't find no marks on these cards," K.C. complained. Mind if I take a look at them?" Joe asked. "Be my guest," K.C. flipped the deck of cards to the speaker. Joe shuffled the deck and passed out one hand to each player. They went through a dozen hands before Joe finely said, "there is the mark." "Where?" K.C. asked looking at the back of his cards, "I don't see nothin." "There is a small dot built into the cards and you can only see it when the light is right. If you don't know what you're looking for it will slip past without ever being seen." "Well, you're good with cards, checkers and guns," the deputy said, "what else are you any good at?" "Well I can ride a horse," Joe said with a smile." "I guess we all know that," Schon said. "It's getting late and I've got to make rounds," Schon said picking up the cards and placing them in the marshal's desk, "we'll finish the checkers later," he told Joe as he left the office. K.C. lay down but he was not sleeping. "How am I gonna get out of this?" kept running through his head but he could not think his way out of the mess he was in. "If I could only get word to my brothers' maybe they could figure me a way out of this mess," K.C. thought as his eyes finally closed in a fitful sleep.

Late that night Joe woke up and began to stretch, he did not want to lose his edge. After the pull ups he got into the gunfighters stance again, it had become so routine to him that he did it without conscious thought, and began to practice his draw. As his hands reached for the imaginary weapons he heard a tapping on the wall of the cell. "K.C." a voice whispered. K.C. woke up, "Who is it?" he whispered back. "It's me, Nicole," she answered. "What are you doing?" he asks. "I'm breaking you out!" "How," he asked. "I'm blowing the window," she replied. "You can't use dynamite, you don't know what you're doing, and you'll blow the jail to pieces and everyone in it!" "That's why I brought Eric; he's an expert with the stuff." Eric's head popped up in the window, "Hi brother," he said as he began to place the explosives in the window. "Why are you doing this? You told your old man you were pregnant. I thought you wanted to marry me?" "I do," she said, but on my terms not his, besides if I had not told him that I was pregnant and thrown such a fit, you would already be dead. He was gonna hang you from the cottonwood tree at the front gate as a warning to the other rustlers roaming the valley." At nineteen the thought of his neck stretching from the limb of the cottonwood did not sound too appealing. "Where is the deputy," K.C. asked Nicole. "He's at the bar, some of the Rocking 'R' riders came in liquored up and ready for trouble, he's down there trying to keep a lid on things." "Get me my gun, it's in the top drawer of the Marshal's desk and my gun belt is hanging on a hook in the office." "No," she replied, "The front door is locked and if we try busting it down everyone in town will hear." "How about my horse, did you bring him?" "Sure did along with a rifle, a canteen and enough grub to last a week." "What about the cattle, are we gonna leave them or do you want to try to sneak them off the old man's place?" "Neither," she said, "Colton and Parker left with the herd you gathered two days ago, by now they are half way to Mexico and they even took the twenty head pa put your brand on!" Eric popped in "you two gonna jaw all night or are we gonna blow this here wall?" Eric cut a two foot section of blasting cord and shoved it into the end of a stick of dynamite. "You best get back!" he said as he struck a match and lit the end of the cord. Eric and Nicole ran around the corner as the cord began to sizzle and pop. K.C. hid in the far corner of the cell trying to protect himself from the blast. "Hey kid, like this," Joe said taking the mattress from his bunk and doubling it then he rolled himself into a ball in the farthest corner of the cell pulling the mattress over his entire body, then he covered his ears with his hands to protect them from the shattering blast that was about to come. K.C. pulled the mattress off his bunk and followed suit. Moments later the roar of the dynamite rocked the room. Pieces of flying brick hammered at the bars of the cell as dust filled the room and drifted to the floor. Eric ran from the corner of the jail and began kicking loose bricks from the jail house wall making the hole even larger. "Come on K.C., we gotta move!" Half stunned from the blast, K.C. managed to get up. "What happened," he asked as Eric climbed through the opening and started to drag him towards the wall. 'Nothing," he screamed, "now let's get going before the whole town gets here." Eric was half lifting and half shoving him into the hole. Nicole grabbed him by the head and began to pull. "Hey, your old man ain't gonna have to hang me," he complained, "you two are gonna do it for him!" "Shut up!" Eric screamed and shoved even harder. Joe threw the mattress off his body with a grimace, every bone in his body felt as if they had been hit by the flying pieces of brick. "The next time you idiots decide to make a jail break, leave me out of it will you!" K.C. still looked groggy, "heck," he said, "next time I hope they leave me out of it!" Eric pushed him the rest of the way through the opening and then dove through himself. "Where are the horses Eric?" Joe heard the voice of the young woman near hysteria. "The dynamite scared them and they ran off!" she cried, "I could not hold them." "Which way did they go?" Eric asked. She must have pointed because Joe heard her say that way and then came the sound of running boots. Joe threw the mattress on the bunk and lay back down, heck anything is possible but he had a better chance of becoming a dirt clod farmer than those three did of making it to Mexico. Joe's head had barley hit the pillow before the jail door was thrown open. Schon, Rog and half a dozen armed men charged into the room, "What happened," he asked. "What does it look like," Joe answered, "you've had a jail break!" "Which way did they go?" Rog demanded glaring at the older man. Joe did not like the hostile attitude of the young deputy and swung to his feet. "How would I know, it's dark outside, I'm locked in a cell and besides that I almost got my head blown off by the blast and a buck board load of bricks!" In two steps Joe was at the bars of the cell, the fire of pent up rage was evident in the hard drawn lines of his face. Schon stepped between the two men, "Alright cool down," he said, "we've got enough trouble already. Rog backed away from the bars, "fine, "he said, "let's just get after the flipping cattle thief." Rog was taking the jail break personal and wanted revenge on any and all responsible. "Not tonight," the voice came from the Marshal standing in the door. "Why not," Rog demanded, "Because all you're going to do at night is stumble around in the dark and mess up any tracks they might have left!" "Then what will we do?" Schon asked, "We just can't stand here!" "Your right," Jim said, "go home and go to bed, you'll need some rest for tomorrow." All of the men left the jail talking about the daring escape by the outlaws.

Early the next morning Joe watched as close to a dozen riders assembled themselves in the Marshal's office, these were cruel vicious men, most of them came from two of the larger cattle outfits and they were the scum of the men who worked there. Most ranchers wouldn't hire them on a bet; all of them carried high powered rifles and pistols that rode in tied down holsters. Some had new rope ready to hang the young outlaws as they caught them. Schon and Rog were in the office also and both men held rifles cradled in their arms as they leaned against opposite walls waiting for the Marshal to come in. Jim listened to the roar of excited men as they swarmed him, impatient to get on with the hunt. The Marshal withdrew a set of pistols from the desk and strapped them on then he took a rifle from the rack, checked the loads and turned around to have a look at the posse. Two of the men were store keepers, the other worked at the stables, "you go home," he said. As the rejected members of the posse left Jim dropped the barrel of the rifle to point directly into the face of one of the men with the rope, "the rest of you can head back to your spread as well, we don't need you." "Hey, we were paid to ride along and were gonna!" one of the men in the posse growled. Jim swung the rifle towards the speaker, "my thumb slips and you will be riding in a pine box!" It was easy to see Jim was in no mood to argue, the white of his knuckles showed that the trigger had already been pulled. Sweat began to appear on the lip of the speaker, "we just wanted to help," he began but Jim cut him off, "like heck you did!" he glared back at them, "you're nothing but a lynch mob and if I catch any of you following me I'll put a bullet in you myself!"

"Now get out!" Several of the riders complained under their breath but none of them wanted to start a war with the lawman or his deputy's.

As the posse broke up and headed back to the ranches that had hired them, Jim began to build a war bag. "When are we leaving?" Schon asked. "You ain't!" Jim replied. "The Rocking 'R' has been pushing cattle into the Malloy place, there's gonna be a blow up pretty soon and I'll need you here to keep a lid on it." "You ain't crazy enough to go after that bunch alone are you?" Rog asked. Jim picked up the keys to the cells, "I guess it's up to him!" Jim was pointing at Joe. "Well you think that black of yours needs to stretch its legs?" Joe sat startled for a moment unable to believe his ear's, "I ain't killen no kid!" Joe shot back at the Marshal. "I ain't asking you to kill anybody, just wanted to know if that back needed to stretch its legs, that's all." Joe shook his head, "I ain't hunting them for you either!" "You can help me find them kids before that lynch mob does or you can let them hang them, it's up to you." Jim just stared at him. Joe began to cuss, "what about the hearing?" Joe asked. The Marshal was getting aggravated, "fine," he said as he started to close the cell door. "I'll go after them myself but if that bunch bushwhacks me or hangs them kids, it will be partly you're fault because you could have helped but wouldn't!" Joe began to cuss again, "alright I'll go!" he said through gritted teeth. Joe hated to admit it but he was kind of fond of the wild eyed cattle thief! Jim threw Joe his gun belt and dug the pistols out of the drawer and handed them to the gunman, "don't shoot yourself with them," he said with a sideways grin. "That's gonna be hard to do seeing their empty!" Joe was not sure if he liked the Marshal or not but he was sure he didn't like the sarcasm! "Well maybe you better load them then," Jim said as he walked out of the office. Joe strapped on the gun belt and began to follow. "What makes you think I won't shoot you in the back and ride off?" Jim stopped and turned around, "I sent telegraphs to every sheriff and marshal in the country, you're a small time rancher from Oklahoma as far as anyone can tell and I don't guess anybody alive has ever seen you pull a gun and those that have ain't around to tell about it! Either way you're clean, plugging me in the back would be kind of stupid if nothing else and I don't think you're stupid! Jim turned into the Crooked Horn with Joe following.

Sherlene and Marilyn were sitting at one of the tables sipping coffee, "hi honey," Jim said and kissed his wife gently on the lips. "Do you think we could get something to go?" Marilyn looked at Joe, "are you leaving?" she asked "Just for a few days," he answered, "I'm riding with the marshal." "You're not hunting those kids are you?" Joe shook his head, "I ain't hunting anyone just taking the black out to stretch his legs." "Good," she said, "I like those kids." "Sis," Jim said, "I think you like just about everybody." "We'll fix you a bag," she said with a giggle in her voice as the two women got up and headed for the kitchen. Joe watched her leave thinking, "I'm in love with a woman that thinks of me as a gunman, a hired killer, and the lowest of the low." Jim shoved a cup of coffee in front of him, "best drink up, the stuff I make will keep you awake for days!" Joe picked up the cup, "how long do you think we'll be gone?" he asked. "Maybe a week, why, you missing her already?" "What are you talking about?" Joe asked. Marilyn of course, a blind man can see how you feel about her." Joe mumbled under his breath, "What would she want with a broken down ex cattle rancher." "What did you say?" Jim asked, knowing full well what he heard. "I didn't say anything," Joe answered. The women came back from the kitchen, Sherlene put the bag down in front of him, "honey will you have time to join us before you go?" "Not really, I figure the Malloy outfit will have men out looking for them and I don't want them to catch that wild bunch of kids before we do." "Why, what do you think will happen," Sherlene asked guardedly, knowing Jim could be risking his life. "I think they will hang them!" Marilyn looked shocked. "Surly they would not hang the girl," she said. "I think they will hang them all." Jim stated flatly. Joe couldn't believe what he was hearing, "nobody would kill their own daughter over a few head of cattle!" "She's not his daughter." Jim said. "Ten or twelve years ago Nicole's real parents had a pretty good spread. A couple thousand head of cattle on five or six thousand acres of prime grazing land, not counting fifty to a hundred head of horses. The plague was going around at the time and they caught it. Nicole was sick for a long time and by the time she came out of it both of her parents were gone. She stayed with a neighbor until her uncle showed up and took over. He has run the place like it was his ever since. He even had the girl call him dad. I guess he was hoping people would forget the ranch rightfully belonged to Nicole. In a few months she will be old enough to take control of the ranch and with the help of that gunslinger of hers she could take control of the ranch maybe even run him off. "If he's all that good how did he get caught in the first place?" Joe asked. Jim could not help but smile, "got caught with his pants down literally." The kid went to the ranch to visit Nicole and while he was there he had to make a trip to the outhouse. Old man Malloy had some of his men staked out watching the place. When the kid sat down one of the hired guns slid a pistol through a knot hole and into the kids back. Told him if he moved he would gut shoot him. The kid had no choice but to set there as the rest of the men took his guns and put a noose around his neck. The only thing that stopped them was Nicole. Told them she would turn them in for murder if they went ahead with their plans." "Any way that was the story I got when I was summoned to the ranch and arrested K.C." "What about the rest of it?" Joe asked. "She even told the old man she was pregnant and the old man really acted upset over that!" "Sure he acted mad," Jim said, "that was just what it was acting. He may have some feelings for the girl but he loves the ranch a lot more and as long as she is alive he can never rightfully own the place. I'll bet he even put the K.C. brand on his own cattle, hoping to frame the kid. The way I see it the quicker she is dead the better he will like it!" Marilyn looked at Joe with a new kind of fear in her eyes. "You won't let that happen will you, "she asked. Joe did not know what to say, but all of a sudden he knew he would die for this woman! "Not as long as I'm alive," he said quietly. Sherlene spoke up "There's a tin of lard in there, a couple hands full of coffee, some beef jerky and a couple slices of bacon. I threw in two slices of blackberry pie and some salt for the both of you." Sherlene sat down beside her husband, "you're not going to bring those kids back are you?" she ask. "It's my job, he stated, but I'll do everything I can to see they get a fair trial." "Yes and if Malloy has his way he will have every cowhand he has got on the jury. He might even manage to get the girl hung for stealing her own cattle," Marilyn said with a cold hot anger flaring in her eyes. "I won't let it go that far," Jim said. Joe's eyes had taken on a darkness of their own. He may not have been a hired gun but the look of a man who knew how to kill was on his face. "Neither will I," Joe said.

Jim finished the last of his coffee, "if we don't want it to happen we better get going," he said. Both ladies watched as the men in their lives walked out the door. Sherlene turned to Marilyn, "sis has a boyfriend, sis has a boyfriend." Marilyn turned red and threw a wet wash cloth at Sherlene, "shut up," she said in mock anger as she headed back into the kitchen.

Jim threw a blanket and saddle on a mule headed roan and backed the animal out of the stall. "Hey, you coming?" he said as Joe threw a rope over the neck of the black. "I'll be there in a minute," Joe answered as he fought the black. "Want me to shoot him for you; it will make him easier to ride!" Joe turned on the Marshal, "you shoot him and you better keep firing because I'll be coming for you!" Jim began to laugh, "Man you been alone too long!" Joe was steaming, "What is that supposed to mean?" Jim shook his head, "nothing, it's just that you don't know a joke when you hear one." Joe realized the marshal was teasing and settled down, "I'll be ready as soon as I get a saddle on this thing," he said. Jim watched as Joe put a saddle on the horse and stepped into the stirrup; the black lowered its head, hunched its back and kicked straight back, and then spun to the left trying to throw the rider. It spun one more time and jumped into the air and landed on its front hooves. Joe's left hand held the reins as his right hand gripped the saddle horn. The force of the impact slammed Joe's head forward as the blacks came back at the same time ramming into Joe's face and the blood began to poor. Joe pulled the reins hard to the left forcing the horse to turn then kicked it hard in the ribs with the heel of his boots letting the animal have its lead. The black took off at a hard run; large clods of dirt flew into the air torn from under the hooves of the animal. Both horse and rider circled the corral before the animal was brought under control. Joe sat wiping the blood off his face as Jim rode up, "you sure you don't want me to shoot that thing," he said again. Joe spit blood from his mouth "one more ride like that and I might shoot him myself!" Jim reached down from the back of the roan and swung the gate open, "we'll stop by the office and get you a badge, I want to make this legal." Joe shrugged, "legal or not I guess I'll ride with you at least until we find the kids." Joe was thinking of the waitress and the soft brown eyes and the thought of having her arms around him, "I made a promise and I plan on keeping it," he said.

The Marshal and the ex-prisoner stepped down in front of the Marshal's office, wrapped the reins of the horses around the hitching post and went in. Schon sat at the desk with his feet propped up on the bars and Rog leaned against the cell bars sipping a cup of coffee, "Don't you two have anything to do?" "Not at the moment," Schon answered, "You know it never gets busy until after dark," Jim looked frustrated, "you ain't gonna hold many prisoners in the condition this place is in. How about putting some bricks back on that wall?" Schon got up and headed for the stove, "we'll get it done before you get back," he said as he took a cup and began to pour himself a cup of day old coffee. "Besides, one cell will work for now cause we ain't ever had that many prisoners." "We're fixing to," Jim said, "so get ready." Rog pushed off the cell bars with a shrug, "I think there is some mortar mix behind the stable, I'll go get it and I'll see if I can find some bricks while I'm at it." Jim opened the desk drawer and took out a silver plated star, "here I guess I need to swear you in," as he handed the badge to Joe. "Do you Joe, what's your last name, I forgot?" "Stroud," he replied. "Do you Joe Stroud; swear to up hold the law to the best of your abilities?" "I do," Joe said as he pinned the badge to his shirt. Joe laid three shells on the marshal's desk, got a straight razor from the shaving kit setting by the pot bellied stove and began cutting deep X's in the top of the soft lead, "Do you really think you're going to need that?" asked Schon. "You never can tell!" Joe replied as he replaced the spent shells of the sawed off forty-four. Jim and the new deputy headed south out of town. Nita and two of her girls were standing out on the balcony as they passed. The two girls were wearing tight silken blouses with some of the buttons open and they were bending over the rail and began yelling at the marshal, "hey, who's the new deputy?" they cried. The Marshal brought the horse to a stop, "Nita, get them girls buttoned up or get them inside before I close the place!" Nita giggled and told the girls to button up and both girls began to laugh, "We can't never have no fun," they complained as they headed inside. "Sorry about that," Nita said, "you know how girls are." "No," Jim said, "I don't, so keep them inside or keep them decent!" "I've got enough trouble at the moment!" Nita turned and went inside, neither of the lawmen paid attention to the man standing in the doorway.

Standing in the doorway it was clear he was no cowboy; dressed in a dark suit and string tie he looked more like a Sunday go to meeting preacher than a gunman. "So that's the man I'm supposed to kill, not much to look at," thought Larry Cheatham, as he went back into the cathouse. Johnny Vasquez had told him about the job, said it paid five hundred dollars to kill a cowboy or two and run the rest out of town, Larry was not the kind to turn down a job and the money was right so he headed for the border town. When he got there he had talked to the owner of the Rocking 'R' ranch, it was owned by a guy named Skip MacCland. Skip was broad shouldered and narrow hipped with hair red enough to show a blood line of the Irish and if looks meant anything a temper to match! He looked mean enough to take care of his own problems. Larry had no idea why he would hire a gun out of Mexico and did not care but Skip had changed his mind, he was no longer interested in the cowboys, he wanted a broken down old cowboy riding a jailhouse bunk bed killed. It didn't make any difference to Larry, besides, it looked like easy money. Pulling a cork from a bottle of fine bourbon whisky Larry headed up the stairs. The one person on earth who knew him and what he did for a living was waiting for him. Trish didn't care about his job she loved him. She had moved here a couple of months ago to help her aunt run this place but she was his and no one else's. This he could depend on.

Around noon the Marshal and Joe picked up the trail of the escaped outlaw's and by the deep cut marks from the hooves of the horses in the hard ground it was easy to tell they were riding fast. "Their gonna kill them mounts," Joe said. "Probably, admitted Jim, we'll just poke along and see what happens." "You ain't in no hurry to catch those kids are you?" "Nope," Said the Marshal. "What if the Malloy bunch catches them?" Joe asked. Jim pulled his horse to a stop, "that's why I brought you." Joe shook his head, "I told you I ain't no gunman!" "Well you better be or we could both wind up being dead, because I ain't one either!" Joe looked the Marshal over real good, "if you ain't a gunman how come you're a Marshal?" "I'm a clod hopping farmer that got voted into the job. I ain't never killed a man in my life and I'm hoping I never have to!" "For a man that's never killed anyone you pulled a pretty good bluff back at the jail." "Yes and I was sweating bullets when I did it! If one of them boys would have pulled leather I'd have shot him alright probably ten times just to make sure he was dead!" Joe shook his head "how did I get into this mess, chasing a bunch of kids to the Mexican border with a Marshal that might not know one end of a gun from the other and a lynch mob out to kill everybody. If I had half a brain I'd ride out of here!" Then Joe remembered the promise to the brown eyed waitress, "Crap," he said to himself, and slapped the black with the reins. Jim choked in the dust as horse and rider took off. "Ain't no way we're gonna catch them old boy," Jim said softly as he leaned forward and patted the roan on the back of the neck, "guess we'll just have to outlast them," and with that he spurred the horse and took off following the dust trail of the black.

"You sure we're on the right trail?" Nicole whined. "You bet," came the reply from the young man riding at her side. "Eric and me have brought ten to fifteen herds down this way." "What about water, we're just about out and my canteens dry!" Nicole continued to whine. "Quit crying, will you there's a spring fed pond below that mountain and we will be there in a few minutes. You can even go swimming if you want." "That ain't much of a mountain, "she stated. "Woman you bellyache about everything. We're half way to Mexico and we've got a decent herd of cattle in front of us and food in our bellies, what more do you want?" I want my ranch," she said, "my mother and father are buried there; they built that place from scratch and now I'm running off and leaving it, I feel like I'm deserting them!" "Fine," K.C. said, "we'll sell the cattle in Mexico, set on the cash for a few months till you're of legal age and then hire some gun's and take the place back by force and if we have to we'll bury your uncle by his brother!" Eric rode up, "it's all clear." "What do you mean all clear?" Nicole wanted to know. "Remember we have the law chasing us because of that little jailbreak, besides that you don't think your uncle is gonna let you ride off do you?"

K.C. said. "He probably has a dozen men hunting us. After all you're the legal heir to the ranch." "My uncle would never harm me!" Nicole said, "He raised me like I was his own daughter." "Sure," K.C. said. "I have no doubt he loves you to a point but he loves that ranch more and now you're old enough to become a threat to him and the ranch. Face the facts honey, this month he can put my brand on one cow and have me hung as a rustler and next month you can give me a thousand head of cattle and there is nothing he can do about it!" "He does not want you to have control of the ranch and he does not want you to have that kind of power!" Nicole rode in silence to the edge of the pond, "did they really think he would go that far?" Nicole pulled the high topped leather riding boots off and hung them from the horn of her saddle using the string from the wide brimmed western hat she wore, would my uncle have me killed? She wondered as she dived into the warm waters of a southwestern Texas pond.

Larry Cheatham got up from the warm bed still half drugged; he was not hung over because some of the Bourbon still surged through his veins. His temper was starting to flair, "don't let anybody touch that," he said as he pointed at the bottle on the dresser. "Sure," Trish said as she wiped the sleep from her eyes and smiled up at him, "Whatever you say honey," and lay back on the pillow watching him. Larry was meticulous in his dress tucking the shirt in making sure the draw string tie was in line with the shirt buttons. Everything had to be perfect for the man who had come from Louisiana, not even the bulge from the short barreled hide out gun under his left shoulder was apparent. Laying a five dollar gold piece on the dresser next to the wash basin Larry said, "I'll be back later" and shut the door as he left. As Trish turned over and tried to go back to sleep she wondered if she would see him again.

Ashley Fry was sweeping off the wooden sidewalk in front of the general store as Larry walked by, something about him caught her attention, laying the broom aside she watched as he crossed the street in the direction of the Crooked Horn restaurant and saloon, she was certain she knew the man. As he walked through the doors of the restaurant Ashley started across the street to the Marshal's office, "Where is the Marshal," she asked as she entered. Schon sat in the Marshal's chair with his feet kicked through the bars of one of the cells, "Him and the gunslinger is out on the trail. His name is Joe and he ain't no gunslinger." Rog cut in as he was placing the last of the bricks in the hole he was repairing from the blast, "He's a rancher from Oklahoma." Rog stepped back and admired his handiwork, "Maybe that will hold until we get a real brick layer in here," he said. Ashley was in a hurry, she had to talk to someone and the deputy's were the only ones there, "Listen, she said, there's a gunman in town, a real gunman, not some broken down cowboy who got lucky!" "I know the man, his name is Larry Cheatham and I've seen him kill men before!" Rog stopped admiring his work and looked over at Ashley, "how do you know it's him and how do you know he's in town?" "I just saw him walk out of Nita's place and it's easy to know it's him. " Ashley looked down embarrassed to admit where she had once worked, "I used to work on the water front," she admitted, "the place was shady, always in trouble with the law, Larry worked there as a bouncer. The tables were rigged but sometimes a river captain or a crew member would get lucky and win big, well you can guess that did not set well with the owner and he would send Larry and a guy named Johnny Vasquez after the lucky winner, only they weren't that lucky any more, Larry and this Vasquez would pistol whip them, drag them into an alley and leave them there. The law got tired of the complaints and began to watch the place, one night there a big winner and after he left, Larry and Vasquez followed him. They weren't happy to just pistol whip him they beat the man to death and left him in the alley. The law found the body and came looking for both of them. I was serving drinks at one of the tables when the officers came to arrest them. Larry said he would go quietly then he grabs that little sneak pistol under his jacket and shoots one man in the face the other officer didn't have a chance, he was facing Vasquez when Larry shot him twice in the back. I heard both Vasquez and Larry headed to Mexico trying to hide from the law. I left Louisiana and came here trying to outrun my past. I didn't want anyone to know what I had been or where I had come from. I bought the store and changed my name, hoping no one would ever find out but I knew the second I saw Larry that I had to tell someone, he is a murderer and he is here to kill someone! With a price on his head he would never take a chance on coming here and getting caught if he were not being paid." Ashley was near hysteria, Schon could feel her body shaking as he put his arm around her shoulders. "I'll walk you home he said and then I want you to take the day off and stay out of sight. If you know him he'll know you, Rog and I will handle this Cheatham fellow, and if we can find a warrant on him we'll arrest him if not we'll keep a watch on him and if he blinks we'll know it." "Just don't let know him know that you told us anything, I don't want him to know we are keeping a watch on him and I don't want him to up and vanish." Rog started going through the old warrants in the Marshal's desk trying to find the picture of a man that fit Larry's description as Schon walked Ashley to her home. "Dang," Rog muttered to himself, "nobody leaves warrants laying around for five or ten years, why couldn't they have come two or three years ago? I can't find anything on Vasquez and I doubt if I'll find anything on this Cheatham fellow either. Schon entered the room and caught the last of Rog's complaint, Fine send a telegraph to a judge or marshal in Louisiana and see if one of them can come up with an expectation warrant. If they can we will arrest the man before the Marshal even gets back, if not we'll wait and see what he wants to do."

Joe pulled back the reins on the black, riding into a small draw as the Marshal and the roan caught up with him. "Slow down fellow, my old horse ain't used to that kind of running." Joe shrugged, "that ain't running, for the black that was a Sunday stroll and why are you riding a broken down nag on a man hunt anyway?" "He ain't that broke down, besides I like him!" Jim stated, "He's sure footed and wakes up every morning in a good mood unlike some people I know." Joe rode the black out on the east side of the draw and turned to the Marshal, "which way?" he asked and Jim pointed, "keep heading east, I figure we'll pick up another set of tracks pretty soon." Joe drew back and slapped the black with the reins again and in a few seconds they were gone throwing a trail of dust and dirt behind them. Joe turned the black heading into another draw and out of sight, "Crap, I might as well be riding alone," Jim thought as he laid the heels of his boots into the roan. Half an hour later a Jim caught up to Joe and the black, this time it was not hard to do, Joe sat in the saddle studying a fresh set of tracks but these weren't the tracks of three riders, they were the tracks of five. "We might as well follow these," the Marshal said, pulling the reins and turning the horse to the south following the new trail. The sun was dropping below the horizon as the Marshal dismounted, "might as well make camp here," he said, "my old nag has about had it, besides it's as good as a camp spot as we will find in this area. Joe swung down from the black and began to remove the saddle and blanket, "think we'll catch those kids before they make Mexico?" He asked. The Marshal pulled the saddle and blanket off his own mount, "yep, the way I see it Eric and Nicole broke K.C. out of jail that left his two cousins out of the play." "They are a tight knit bunch and where you see one or two you'll see the others also. The only way they would not have been there helping was if they were busy someplace else." "So where do you think they were?" Joe asked. "Well I think they are taking a herd of cattle across the border. They probably started off before the jail break; it's got to be a small herd if it's just the two of them driving it. K.C. and the rest will try to catch up with them on this side of the border, if not they will meet them on the other side, not a big deal either way." "What about the trail we're following, Joe asked, where do you figure they fit into the deal?" "Men from the MacCland outfit or the Malloy ranch, maybe both riding together, as neither one wants the girl to take over the ranch," Jim said. "One thing's for sure, it will be the scum of the outfits, men that will kill a woman as easy as a man. They will try to catch them on the Mexican side of the border and bushwhack them and drive off the cattle making it look like a simple rustling job gone bad. They might even bury the bodies hoping no one will ever find out what they've done." Jim took out the makings and began to role a cigarette as Joe gathered some dry limbs from a mesquite tree to build a fire. After placing a match in the brush pile Joe reached over and picked up the tobacco, I always heard a lawman's not allowed to cross the border, some kinds of agreement between the U.S. and Mexico, but you're planning on us crossing over anyway ain't you?" Jim shrugged his shoulders, "unless you got some kind of objection," Joe thought about it shrugged his shoulders and said "I ain't the one who's gonna lose my job." After placing some rocks around the fire Jim picked up a large cast iron skillet and placed it over the fire, filled it half full of water and added a hand full of coffee grounds, "Besides the gambler, you ever killed anyone before?" Jim asked. Joe had a haunted look as he stared into the campfire, "I was in the war," he said. Joe never said which side he fought for or how many battles he had been in or how many he had killed, he seem as if he was suddenly somewhere else. Jim studied the clothes of the man trying to figure out which side he had fought for, an emblem, a rank, or anything that connected him to the service but he finally gave up, he couldn't find anything on Joe that showed if he had fought for the north or the south or if he was an officer or foot soldier.

Placing his handkerchief over a tin cup worked as a filter to keep the grounds out as Joe poured a cup of coffee. No one had to tell him it was going to be bitter, he had never tasted a decent cup of coffee that had been boiled over a campfire. Pouring the last of the liquid on the ground he laid some bacon in the skillet and placed it back on the fire, "if you don't think they will try anything until after they cross the border why don't we ride ahead and wait for them to come to us?" "That's kind of what I was thinking, Jim admitted, I just wanted to hang back long enough to find out how many we were going to have to deal with." Joe shoved the stirrup under the saddle and spread his bed role and then took a biscuit out of the bag Marilyn had packed. Joe tore it open and placed some of the bacon between the slices and began to eat hungrily. "See you in the morning," he said as he pulled his hat down over his eyes and chewed on the biscuit. "Great, he runs off and leaves me all day with no one to talk to but my horse and now he falls asleep like I don't exist!" Jim spread his bed role and lay back staring at the stars, "I would rather be home with my wife," he thought as his eyes closed and he fell asleep. That night as Jim slept Joe got up from the homemade bed and snuck out of camp. He was bare footed but felt it was better to step on a snake than to awaken the Marshal. Fifty to a hundred yards from camp he stopped and began the nightly ritual, first he began to draw with one hand then the other, turning his left hand palms out drawing from the cross draw position, getting faster and faster with each draw. It felt good to be working with the pistols again and not grabbing empty air. "Can you hit like that?" even before the words were finished Joe had spun around dropped into the gunfighters stance and crouching low with the knees bent as the right hand hovered over the hammer ready to fan in a moment's notice, the pistol in Joe's left hand was pointed at the center of the Marshal's chest, the hammer was drawn back and ready to fire. Jim swallowed hard and even in the cool night air Jim knew he was beginning to sweat, he had never been this close to death. "Don't let that hammer slip," he said looking into the barrel of the forty-four, knowing the only thing standing between life and death was the weight of the thumb holding the hammer back. The barrel of the revolver lifted as the hammer lowered. "That's a good way to get your head blown off!" Joe said as he placed the gun back into the holster. "I thought you weren't a gunfighter," Jim said trying to shake the feeling of doom that had settled on him after staring into the barrel of the forty-four. Joe held a look of rage and said, "And I did not think you were an idiot!" Part of the anger was from the fact he had almost killed an innocent man and partly because he had let another man sneak up behind him. Both men glared at each other in the dark of the night.

Paul stood behind the bar polishing a beer glass as Larry Cheatham walked in. Paul was thinking, "If I could save enough money I could buy the women out and if I was the owner I could rip out the kitchen and maybe bring in a couple of Nita's girls. I could really make some money then!" Lost in the day dream, Paul paid no attention to his new customer. Larry was growing impatient even as he walked to the table. The whisky he had consumed the night before still gnawed at his belly. "Hey you wake up," as he sat at a table. Bring me a beer and a waitress," Larry ordered hoping the alcohol and food would settle the queasy feeling he had in the pit of his stomach. Paul brought the beer and set it in front of the customer, "A waitress will be here in a second," he said as he went back to his day dream. Sheila came bouncing up like a school girl, giddy at the thought of a large tip, after all the man was dressed in a fine suit and showed the makings of a gentleman. "What will it be?" she asked with a big smile on her face thinking "Maybe this was the man who was going to take her away from the life of a waitress. She was tired of standing on her feet all day listening to the drunken cowboys whooping it up at the bar and she was tired of cleaning the dung off the floor as they made their way to the restaurant. One day she planned to marry but she wanted a man that had never punched cattle or dug in the ground to plant a crop. She wanted a man of style one who knew what an opera was and not a man who's idea of a night on the town consisted of listening to a half dressed woman sing buffalo gal won't you come out tonight or shooting cow chips from a fence post by the light of the moon! She was hoping and praying this was that man. "Give me some fried potatoes, eggs and a cup of coffee," Larry said finishing the last of the beer. Sheila turned quick flinging her skirt as she did showing a flash of leg and the smile she wore left no doubt this had been done on purpose.

Paul brought the coffee and placed it on the table in front of the man in the suit, "Heck if I had a suit like that maybe Sheila would be flirting with me," Paul thought as he went back to the bar. "One day I'm gonna buy me one and find out." Paul had absolutely no hope; he was big and ugly with a scar running down his face, a bartender's mentality and a bad temper. None of the waitresses wanted anything to do with him. They dreamed of the day when they could buy his share of the restaurant and close the bar and drive the drunks out of the place and be rid of the bad tempered bartender for good. Sheila brought the meal Larry had ordered to his table and set them down and pulled a chair up for herself, "Where do you hail from?" she asked as she sat across from him. Larry studied the young waitress, she would never know if he lied. "Chicago, Illinois," he said but this was no lie, Larry had been born in Chicago and lived most of his life in the streets and back alleys of the Great Lakes water fronts. He killed his first man there, it had not been a fair fight, the man staggered out of one of the local taverns too drunk to walk, and Larry walked up behind him and slid a knife in his back. He would have gotten away with it too if he was a lucky man but he wasn't. One of the man's friends had come out of the bar looking for him and saw Larry with the knife in his hand as the man started to yell. People came out of the bar with clubs and knives ready to avenge their fallen comrade; he barely managed to out run the lynch mob that night and the next day he moved to Louisiana trying to escape the law and the mob hoping no one would find out about his past but back alleys and water front's were in Larry's blood and it didn't take long before he was back in the alleys and saloons waiting for another victim. Larry knew he was good with a knife or a gun and killing a man or a woman meant no more to him than dealing from the bottom of the deck or using loaded dice! Sheila set at the table watching as he sopped up the last of the eggs with a biscuit, "I would take a little more coffee," he said as he wiped at the plate. Sheila got up and swung her skirt again trying to show even more of the young slender legs she was so proud of. She went to the pot belly stove and picked up the hot pot of coffee eager to serve the man she wanted so desperately to know and as she was returning to the table Mike and Roy came through the swinging doors, both men looked as if they had just been stomped on by a charging bull! Roy walked up to the bar and removed two cups, "we'll have some of that," he said as they sat at the table nearest the kitchen. Sheila poured both men a cup of the mud and carried the pot to Larry's table. After pouring him a cup she sat back down eyes shining at the thought of being with a real gentleman. Roy knocked on the kitchen door, "Marilyn" he said his voice barely above a whisper. There was no answer so he knocked again even louder, Mike held his head as the knocking continued, "Not so loud!" he complained, "my head is killing me!" Roy tried to smile through blood shot eyes, "that will teach you to mix bad whisky with day old beer!" he said winching through the pain in his own head. Marilyn came to the door, "What do you two want?" she said irritated at the behavior of the two men. Mike laid his head on the table, "Please not so loud!" he whispered, "My head is going to explode." Marilyn slapped the table with the palm of her hand and the room echoed from the force of the blow. Mike sat up as if he had been shot, winching in pain. "What will you have!" she repeated even louder laughing inwardly at the misery the boys had brought on themselves. Roy answered, "biscuits and gravy and tell Terry please no lumps in the gravy, my stomach could not handle them this morning!" Marilyn left the boys to their misery as she went back into the kitchen. Marilyn screamed at the top of her lungs, "biscuits and gravy and please hold the lumps, their poor little old bellies can't take them this morning," she was laughing at the thought of the men cringing from the sound of her voice. She wore a big smile as she winked at Eloise and began to bang pots and pans knowing the pain she was inflecting in the young cowboys. Later Marilyn came out of the kitchen to find the men had taken their cups and moved to the far corner of the restaurant away from the banging and clatter of the kitchen. Marilyn walked up and slammed the metal plates on the table, "where's your other partner," she asked more to torment and annoy the young men than out of any real curiosity she might have had. "He went out hunting last night and we ain't seen him since," Roy answered. It was Marilyn's turn to be upset, "are you two nuts!" she screamed, "you let a drunken man go hunting in the middle of the night by himself!" Roy and Mike both began to laugh even through their pain, "heck," Mike said, "He went hunting that new girl that went to work at Nita's place last night and besides even if we found him I don't think he was gonna let us drag him home!" "Yeah," Roy put in; he has eyes for that little skirt! "I think her name is Michelle." Marilyn turned and walked away from the table red faced and angry, "one of these days I am gonna learn not to talk to this trio of rowdy cowboys." Even in their hung over state they had gotten the better of her!"

"Who are the jokesters?" Larry asked of the blond haired waitress sitting across from him. Sheila wanted to please the man in front of her and this was her chance, the older one is Roy, the other is called Mike. One of their partners is missing his name is Bobby. They like to come in here and give Marilyn a hard time whenever they get a chance." "Why?" Larry asked. "Don't rightly know, I think those boys all secretly like each other but they don't want the other to know, and as far as Marilyn is concerned I think they wish she was their mother. They know how far they can go before she smacks them."

Larry leaned back in his chair, "so these were the men he had come up from Mexico to gun down or run off," he said to himself. They were young and reckless and true they carried tied down pistols but for most cowboys now days it was more for show than anything else. They might take a shot at a snake or lizard once a month then they would probably miss! Larry doubted if they ever practiced with them and even if they did, it would not be more than a few minutes a week. Like most cowboys they were more at home with a rope or a whip. "Heck, it would be easy money, maybe later he might still be able to pick up a few extra dollars after he took care of the saddle tramp!"

Sheila almost squealed in delight as Larry laid a five dollar gold piece on the table, "keep the change," he said as he got up and walked towards a group of men playing cards. Sheila was all smiles as she picked up the gold piece and slid it into her pocket. It took Nita's girls all week working day and night to earn that much money and she had made it in a few minutes!

Roy and Mike finished their breakfast and as they were getting up to leave Larry was sitting down at the card table, "Deal me in," he said watching for any reaction from the men playing. "After this hand," the voice was that of the dealer. Four cards already lay in front of the men playing, "Sure," Larry answered, knowing full well he could not start in the middle of a hand. They were playing five card draw and Larry studied every hand as they played. He was not watching the cards each were dealt but looking at the hands of the players. They were the hard calloused hands of a working man. The hands of men who tore rocks out of the ground and carried them across the fields, who fought the handles of plows and held tight the leather reins of the plow horses that fell timber for a living. They used doubled bladed axes and played tug of war at the end of a strong rope with half wild cattle and horses. These men dug fence post holes with a long handled shovels and strung barbed wire down the fence line with the barbs digging deep into the leather gloves they wore, tearing away at the flesh and muscle beneath. These were men of strength and character; they were not the soft nimble hands of a gambler. Larry studied the faces of the men playing as well looking for any sign of a professional gambler but found none. They were tanned with rough leather like texture to the skin. "These men would not know a marked deck if I used a pick axe to mark them with," Larry thought as the dealer began to shuffle the deck. Only after studying the men, did Larry look at the deck of cards; they were exactly what he thought they would be, marked, not on purpose but by time. Some of them had faded while others had small nicks or cuts. These cards looked as if they had ridden in a saddle bag at one time or another. Some cowboy had spent a lot of lonely nights playing solitaire with them and it showed. Larry had grown up in water front saloons and in twenty minutes he would know every little nick in the pack and which nock went to which card. Maybe he would throw a few hands making the suckers think they had a patsy. After thirty minutes of playing and Larry had won his second hand Bobby walked into the room like a young man with the world at his finger tips. He sat at the table nearest the kitchen and banged on the wall with his fist and yelled, "hey mom!" at the top of his lungs. Marilyn came into the room like her dress was on fire, "What do you want!" she said clearly angry at the young man. Bobby answered, "Biscuits and gravy please," with a heartwarming smile. "I guess you want me to hold the lumps right?" she spat at him. "Now why would I want you to do that?" Bobby said, "If you did that I would not get any gravy!" Marilyn went into the kitchen and threw a pot against the wall, "Sometimes those boys make me want to bang my head into the wall or better yet their heads!" she grumbled at Eloise. She then picked up the order and walked back to the table, "here!" she hissed placing food in front of Bobby. 'Why aren't you hung over like your buddies?" she asked. "Because that little old girl wouldn't let me drink whisky in bed!" he complained. "Poor Bobby," Marilyn said trying to get the better of the lone cowboy, "I bet she even made you take off your spurs!" "Yes!" Bobby said, "But I didn't mind, she was a right pretty girl!" Marilyn's face turned beet red as she turned and walked back into the kitchen. Eloise watched as Marilyn began to slam her head into the wall," when will I learn?" She said over and over.

Jim woke up to the sounds and smell of bacon frying in the pan, "Dang that smells good," he said as Joe handed him a cup of hot coffee, "You believe in sleeping late, don't you?" Joe asked as he began rolling up his bed. Jim took a sip of the coffee and pulled some of the bacon from the pan and slid it between two halves of a day old biscuit, "If I thought these things were hard yesterday," he complained taking a large bite out of the bread. "Quit complaining and let's go, I'm in a hurry to get to the border." Joe placed the saddle on the back of the black and began to tighten the cinch, "What's the hurry Jim asked, chewing on a tough piece of the bacon. "I want to get to the border before the rest of them do. I'd like to be able to scout the area before they arrive and figure out the best place for an ambush to take place. Maybe even find a place where we can pull an ambush of our own without getting our heads shot off!" Jim threw the last of biscuit in the fire and began kicking sand into the flames, "Great, the first thing I wanted to do this morning was jump out of bed and make a mad dash for the border, why can't people get up at a descent time anyway," Jim complained mockingly as he put the saddle on the roan. Joe sat in the saddle watching as Jim tightened the cinch, "Your right," he said "that horse does get up in a better mood than some people I know." Jim threw his leg over the saddle, "Oh shut up and let's go," he said digging the spurs on his boots into the side of the animal. Joe drew back the reins of the black and gave him a slap and within second Jim was left behind just him and his horse, "I hate that horse," Jim said as he once again found himself riding in the dust trail of the black.

Rick Yarlboro hated his life, he hated camping and he hated the men he was with, in fact he hated everything and everyone. "Get up you bunch of idiots, we ain't got all day!" he growled, kicking at the feet of the man next to him. The Mexican called Frankie sat up in a bad mood of his own, "back off! He warned "We ain't planning nothing until we reach the border and I ain't had any coffee yet!" Rick may have hated every man he was with but he knew better than to cross the Mexican. The so called posse consisted of the scum of both outfits, three of men were from the Rocking 'R' and two from the Malloy ranch. They all had one order from the boss; they were to follow the young outlaws into the Mexican desert and bushwhack the small group and bury the bodies. Rick knew that Skip MacCland hated Don Malloy with a passion but it only made sense that a common bond had brought the men together. Maybe when this was over he would find out what that bond was and who knows, maybe he could use it to his advantage. Until then he had to put up with men like Frankie. One thing he knew Frankie would never face him with a gun, Frankie was a knife fighter and a sneak, and he would just as well cut a man's throat in his sleep as face him! One day he might blow the back of Frankie's head off but until then he had to sleep with one eye open. "Maybe I ought to kill the Mexican now," Rick was thinking as he watched the back of the man sipping coffee Frankie turned and looked back, "did you sleep good amigo?" he asked. It was as if he could read the thoughts of the man behind him. Looking into the face of the Mexican made him nervous. Rick knew the answer before he asked but he had to do or say something to shake the queasy feeling growing in his stomach, "Did you ever kill a man?" Rick asked. The Mexican began to take on a lost look, it was as if he was enjoying the memories, "Si, amigo, many times!" he replied. "Did you ever kill a woman?" Rick persisted. This time the Mexican pulled the heavy Bowie knife from the scabbard on his belt and began to slide his thumb along the blade. Rick had seen this look before, it reminded him of a snake just before it strikes, "Si, amigo, with the knife!" he said staring at the blade. "it does not bother you to kill a woman?" Rick asked. "Man, woman it makes no difference, sometimes the woman, she screams a little more," Frankie said still playing with the edge of the blade.

Rick put a saddle on the bronco he was riding. Once he had been a top hand and a real cowboy but by now he had been busted up too many times. He was old and tired and he could not wrestle the young strong calves anymore or spend days in the saddle. Now he knew why the owner of the Rocking 'R' had kept him around, he was considered one of the scum, a man to send on the trash missions, a man that would do whatever he was told. "If I was younger I'd ride out of here," he thought as he mounted the horse and rode south towards the Mexican desert. Frankie slid the Bowie knife back into the scabbard, "Let us ride amigo," he said rising as he spoke. "We have a busy day today, yes?"

Larry woke up early that morning he had a busy day planed. "Get off me!" he said slapping the leg of the girl sleeping next to him, both were still half groggy from the whisky they had consumed the night before. "Leave me alone!" Trish said rolling over to get away from the abuse. Larry stood in front of the mirror admiring his reflection, "Today is going to be a great day," he thought as he combed his hair. He was down a couple of hundred dollars at the poker tables but that did not matter, he had his sucker cowboys lining up to set at his table hoping to get their hands on some of the free money. Today it was his turn, he was going to take them for every nickel they had. Larry slid the hide out pistol in place and pulled the jacket over it making sure the bulge from the handle didn't show.

Paul pulled a glass from under the bar and filled it from the tap, "here's your breakfast," he said setting the cold beer in front of the gambler. Picking up the glass, Larry studied the room; men were already at the card tables but they were the small time players, men who played for nickels and dimes, he wanted the real players, men who would bet their lives on the flip of a card. Sheila brought a cup of coffee and set it in front of him, "What can I get you?" she asked, still remembering the five dollar tip. Larry took his eyes off the game long enough to smile at the waitress, "I'll have steak and eggs with fried potatoes." Sheila turned and tried to flip her skirt even more than last time, it never hurt to advertise and she could use another five dollar gold piece. Larry watched the game as he waited for breakfast, it would be easy to pick up a few dollars but it was not worth the risk. Sheila brought the meal and a cup of coffee for herself then sat down at the table across from him. Larry was too deep in thought to pay the waitress any attention, "Are you gonna be here long?" she asked trying to draw the man's attention back to her. "No, not long," he said as he slid another five dollar gold piece across the table and got to leave. Sheila wanted to know more about the man but he was in no mood to talk, Larry had seen a sucker come through the doors and he wanted to be the one to fleece him. Taking a deck of cards from his jacket pocket, Larry began to set up a game of solitaire at one of the card tables, "let the suckers come to you," he thought as he began to flip the cards over.

 Frankie kicked dirt at the campfire as the rest of the men saddled their horses; Frankie felt at home with these men, they were men like him, cruel and vicious, all except Rick. Frankie could not stand the sight of the man. Rick was a decent enough kind of man that had hit on hard times. He was not a cold hearted murderer did not belong with the kind of men Frankie liked to ride with. "One day he might slit his throat as he slept," Frankie thought as he threw his leg over the mount.

 Rick could not help but shutter at the thought of the Mexican behind his back. He may not be able to use a pistol but anyone could use a rifle. Rick pulled his mount over to wait for the rest of the men, "Mi amigo," Frankie said as he rode up, "you decided to wait for us that is good, si?" "One day I'm going to have to kill this guy!" Rick decided, "Before he kills me!" "Si mi amigo," he said, "I decided to wait for my friend," as he pulled his horse up next to Frankie's. Together they rode a circle around the herd of cattle and the men they had been following.

Skip MacCland placed two cards on the table and Don Malloy followed suit. The store keeper and the banker had already dropped out of the hand. Larry knew Skip held two pair of kings and sixes. Don was bluffing with a pair of nines; this was the kind of game Larry lived for. Larry dealt two cards to Skip and watching the reflection on the table Larry knew the ace and the four would do him no good. Malloy received a queen and a three, no help for the pair of nines. Skip raised a hundred dollars and Malloy matched the bet and raised another hundred, Larry fumbled with his cards not sure if he should match the bet or fold. There was a lot of money on the table three deuces was not a strong hand but it would beat any the other held. Larry matched the bet and called, Skip took the loss with grace, folded the money in front of him and stood up, "that finished me!" he said as Larry pulled in the pot and started to fold the bills. "Where are you going?" Malloy asked fuming at the thought that Larry was leaving too and with his money. "No use staying," Larry said, "MacCland is out of the game and the money is gone!" Malloy pulled a wad of bills from his shirt pocket and threw them on the table, "sit down!" he instructed, "I want a chance to win my money back. This is what Larry wanted, what he had hoped someone stupid enough and mad enough to bet everything he owned on the flip of a card! When it was Larry's turn to deal Malloy was going to lose everything he owned! The banker and the store keeper had already stepped out of the game and Skip was out as well, this was going to be a game of one on one. In his enraged state Malloy had lost all sense of reason and played the game like an amateur, betting high on a single pair trying to bluff his way through and Larry knew the man was bluffing and bet even higher building the pot. Spectators circled the table watching the amateur lose hand after hand to the professional. Skip MacCland was no coward and no idiot, he knew Larry was a gunman and he had found out the hard way that he was a card shark. Skip was good with a gun but he did not think he could beat Larry in a fair fight so bowing out of the game seemed like the smartest thing to do. Malloy was not that smart, he was throwing good money after bad in an attempt to win what he lost. With every hand Malloy became more and more reckless. Like the rest of the spectators Skip watched as the pile of money in front of Malloy dwindled to nothing. With a scream, Malloy jumped up from the table, the movement was so fast the chair behind him flipped over and crashed to the floor. The long barrel of his revolver was starting to clear the holster as Larry's right hand went for the hide out pistol under his left shoulder. The shots almost sounded like one as fire erupted out of the short barrel of Larry's pistol moments before the flame and lead flew from the longer barrel of the revolver. Malloy may have had nothing more than a mild concussion as the heavy lead from the short gun struck him a glancing blow along the forehead sending blood, flesh and hair flying as the shell dug a shallow trench along his skull. Malloy's head slammed to the right as his own bullet tunneled its way into the thick wooden card table in front of him. Larry's hand fanned the hammer of the short barreled gun and two more flashes of flame erupted from the barrel as lead slammed into Don Malloy's chest, shattering the bone and gristle as they made their way into his heart. No one knows if Malloy felt the sledge hammer like blows to the chest as the bullets passed through his body or if he was even awake as he lay on his back staring at the ceiling above. Larry ejected the spent shells from the pistol and started to replace them when he felt the cold steel of the gun being pressed into his back! He could even feel the sight on the barrel that dug into his flesh, "you even breath and you're dead!" Rog said. The cocking of the hammer sounded like the beating of a drum to Larry's ears. Schon ran through the door with his own pistol in his hand. "Nobody moves!" he shouted. Covering the room under different circumstances Rog would have laughed at the older man but he knew there was a cold blooded killer in his sights and was glad for any help he could get. "Cover him," Rog said as he reached around Larry and took the revolver from his hand. "Let's go!" Rog said shoving him towards the swinging doors. "What about my money?" Larry said starting to turn towards the table. "You touch it you die!" The cold tone in the young deputy's voice told Larry all he needed to know. The young man was walking on egg shells and the slightest move and the gambler knew he was going to die. "Paul, gather up the money and bring it to the jail!" Schon instructed, "The rest of you men drag the body down to the undertakers." "Marilyn has got enough problems around her without him bleeding all over the floor!" Men were lifting the body even as the two deputies escorted the gunman out of the room. Schon locked the cell door as Larry stretched out on the bunk, "you can't hold me and you know it!" "There was a whole room full of witnesses including the deputy," he said as he turned over to wait.

Joe sat on the black staring across the river, "What do you think?" Jim asked watching the man in front of him. "I think they will want to be ten miles on the other side of the border before they try anything," Joe answered. "They won't want a border patrol from either side to hear the battle or to come across the bodies. That will mean pushing the cattle two more days." "What will we do between now and then?" Jim asked. Joe looked at the Marshal, "you really was a clod hopping farmer weren't you!" "Well I said I was didn't I?" Jim said "What did you expect?" "We scout the area and find the best place for an ambush and then we find the best place to ambush the ones pulling the ambush." "That won't take two days, will it?" Jim asked. "No," Joe replied, "we have two days, the kids bringing the cattle in will be here by then and they have been here before or they would not be bringing them into a desert like this. They know where the water is and they will know every nook and draw within a fifty mile radius. They will hide the herd in those draws as they move them deeper into Mexico. Some of the men following them will know the area just as well as they do and some may have even been born here. We have two days to learn as much as we can about the terrain, where the watering holes are and the best way to drive a herd of stolen cattle." "We need to find out where they are likely to pull an ambush without the Federalies or the Rangers finding the bodies or hearing the gunfire." "So let's get moving," Joe said, "we have two days to find out what most men couldn't find out in a month!" With that Joe slapped the black with the reins and started across the river, soon they would be in Mexico. Jim watched the back of the rider in front of him and wondered again who he really was. He was certainly a leader of men as he has shown here. Jim was curious and was willing to let Joe lead. He had a feeling there was a lot more to this man than he wanted anyone to know! Jim spurred his horse and thoughtfully followed the black.

Skip MacCland had never been so angry in his life. True he hated Don Malloy, he even dreamed of the day when he could put a bullet in the man but he did not want it to be today. Skip watched as the men carried Malloy's body out of the Crooked Horn. "Maybe it won't be so bad," he thought, remembering the men he and Malloy had sent out to kill the girl and her companions. With Malloy dead and the girl out of the picture the Malloy ranch would go up for sale or be auctioned off by the county, either way he could pick the ranch and the cattle up cheap! No one in the area had the funds to bid against him and even if they did his men would see to it they didn't! The only thing that stood between him and owning all the grazing land in the valley was the three young cowboys!

Marilyn was tired of the killing, tired of the drunks and tired of dealing with men like Paul and she was going to get rid of them all! "How much do you want for your share of the restaurant?" she asked the blond haired giant. Until that moment Paul had never thought of selling his share of the restaurant, he had his own dreams. With a thousand dollars he could build his own bar with one of those fancy mirrors brought out from back east and faro tables, heck he could even build a couple of extra rooms for some of the girls he would hire, he might even compete with Nita's business. "I want a thousand dollars," he said, "and the mirror over the bar." It was high, more than twice what his share was worth but Marilyn just turned and said, "I'll be back later," as she went out the door on her way to the bank. She hated to borrow money but it would be worth it to be rid of the killing.

The sun was setting below the horizon as Joe swung down from the black, "We'll camp here," he said as he was un-cinching the saddle and letting it slide to the ground. "There is better grass on the north side of the hill," Jim said still sitting on his own mount. "You want a cold camp?" Joe asked as he gathered small pieces of wood to build a fire. "What do you mean?" Jim asked swinging down from the roan. "I mean the hill will hide the light of the fire. If we camp on the other side we have a cold camp or the flames will be seen for miles so it's here or a cold camp, the choice is yours." Jim liked the idea of hot food in his belly, "I guess we'll camp here," he said, pulling the cooking pot from the war bag behind his saddle.

Frankie had the same idea only they were on the north side of the river following the herd of cattle. Sipping from the hot metal cup he watched Rick as he stripped the saddle from his horse, "Coffee, mi amigo?" he said as Rick walked up to the fire, "Maybe tonight I kill him?" Frankie thought as he handed the pot over to the man in front of him. Rick hated the men he rode with and especially the Mexican named Frankie! When this is over he was going to keep on riding and California was sounding good, maybe he would try his luck in the goldfields. Rick leaned his saddle against the butt of a dead stump, maybe no one would notice the alarm system he was building as he kicked the dried out limbs in a circle around the area where he was going to make his bed. Rick pulled the pistol from his belt and held it in his hand as he threw the blanket over his body. But somebody did notice! The Mexican watched with the eyes of a man seeing his plans destroyed. It was as if Rick was reading his mind. Tonight Rick would sleep with one eye open, there was no reason for anyone to walk near the sleeping man and if a twig so much as snapped Rick would come up firing. Frankie would have to come up with a different plan if he wanted to get rid of him!

Joe sat across from the fire and watched as Jim chewed on a hard tack biscuit, he admitted he was no gunman; heck he could barely read signs and did not know how to set up camp. "Why would a man like this become a marshal?" he wondered. Finely his curiosity got the better of him, "Why did you become a Marshal?" he asked. "Didn't have any choice," Jim stated, "I had a good crop in the ground and everything was going great for the first time in my life. I was going to be able to pay everything off and be out of debt. I planned on marrying Sherlene and expanding, maybe buy a larger piece of land and get out of farming. Maybe buy a few head of cattle and go into ranching. I had my life all planned out but a fire came through and burned me out, the house the barn everything. If I was going to stay in the valley I had to find a job. I'm no cowboy and I'm no banker, for me this was the only job open! "What's so important about staying in the valley?" Joe asked, even in the darkness Joe could see the crimson color come to the

Marshal's face. "Sherlene did not want to leave her family and there was no way I was going to leave her, the Marshal's job was open and I took it." "What about you?" Jim asked. "Nothing much to tell, I was a rancher in Oklahoma." "That is not what I meant! What I am trying to find out is how you came to have that monster under you?" Jim said pointing at the black. "Not much to it," Joe said, "I just through a rope around his neck!" "Even I ain't stupid enough to believe that!" Jim said. Joe shrugged, "To tell the truth I sold the ranch and what cattle I had and was on my way to the gold fields in California when I came across the black, he was leading a herd of wild horses. The minute I saw him I knew the gold fields would have to wait. That old horse of mine would never have caught up to the black and even if it did that monster would have killed him so I started to follow the wild herd. Chris-crossing in front of them and letting them catch my scent, letting them get used to the idea that I was around. I would ride up wind anything to let them know I was there. The one thing I had plenty of was time so day after day I circled the herd getting closer every day. When they spooked and ran I just followed the tracks until I caught up. After a while they got used to me and let me get close enough to reach out and touch some of the horses but I never could get close enough to the black to throw a rope and even if I did he would have kicked my horse out from under me so I bided my time cause I knew one day he would make a mistake and I would be there." "What kind of mistake did he make?" Jim asked. "He went swimming!" Joe said, "That's all it took!" "One day he started across a river and when he was about half way there I rode up and pitched my rope as quick as I could and I tied that rope to a good sized sapling, then I threw another rope around his neck, he could not make the other bank with two ropes around his neck and treading water so he turned around and headed back. I kept pulling him down river with my old horse until I had both ropes snugged up then I tied the second rope to another tree. Those trees had enough give to keep him from choking himself but still managed to keep the ropes tight. I built a make shift corral right there around the black and there was nothing he could do about it! After I put a saddle on him we went at it, right there in the middle of that corral!" Jim shook his head, "That is a lot of work for one horse!" "Yes,"

Joe said looking deep in thought remembering how many times the black had thrown him, how many times he had tried to stomp him and how many times he had to force himself to climb back into the saddle knowing that one hard jump, one twist or kick could snap his back like a twig! "I knew I could be thrown and stomped and I would have spent my last few days suffering and alone, my only company the animal that had killed me but he was worth it!" he said with admiration at the black. Jim could not believe anyone would risk his life for a horse, any horse but to risk you life for the stick of dynamite Joe rode was beyond belief or reason! Jim pulled the rifle from his scabbard and laid it beside his saddle, "see you in the morning," he said as he spread his bed role. Joe walked over and gave the black a pat on the neck, "Some people just don't understand!" he said as he rubbed the top of the horses head. The black stepped forward shoving Joe with its shoulder and Joe pushed back with his hands shoving against the horse as hard as he could, the black stopped and swung its head slugging Joe like a battering ram, "Their going to kill each other!" Jim thought as he watched the combatants at play. Joe slapped the black on the neck, "I'll see you in the morning old friend," he said as he turned and walked in the dark towards his own bed. Jim lay with his head on the saddle, "No wonder other horses shied away from the black, the thing was more wild than tame. Its spirit had never been broken and no man had ever ridden the black until it had given up to Joe." Laying there in the dark of the night Jim realized the black had let the man ride him. Somewhere in the mists of the battles they had become friends. It had let Joe ride him because they were two of a kind, kindred spirits, both made of flint and iron and fire. Jim felt a shutter go through his body, he would hate to be the one these two were hunting! As Jim watched, Joe kicked a shallow layer of sand over the fire, filled the skillet full of water and placed it over the pile of sand.

K.C. walked around camp kicking the feet of the sleeping men, "Get up," he was saying, "We got a long ways to go!" Colton and Parker both pulled the cover over their heads, they were tired and worn out, "We've been pushing these cattle for a week!" they complained, "While you been lying around in a jail cell so leave us alone!" Nicole turned on her charms and her smile, "Come on boys!" she began, "We have to make the border today." She had finely come to the realization that her uncle would have men coming for them and that their lives could be in real danger even her own! "Please!" she begged, "Get up and help us move the herd!" her voice had cracked and tears were in her eyes. She knew in the back of her mind her uncle was planning to have her killed. Colton and Parker hated to leave the warmth of the blankets but they finally managed to drag themselves up. Shoving the blankets aside they headed for the fire, a cup of coffee sounded good before starting the daily drive. Parker didn't wait for the hot beverage he threw his saddle over the back of his mount, "Let's get going if we're going to!" he said as he cracked the whip and started the cattle down the draw. Parker knew it would not be long before the others caught up with him and Eric was already pulling the cattle into something that resembled a herd.

If you have never been stabbed it's hard to explain the feel of the knife as the tip of it cuts through the soft layers of skin covering the body, the feeling of the cold metal as it slices through muscle and veins, even the feel of the blade is hard to explain as it grinds like a hacksaw against bone and gristle. It may be hard to believe but you can even hear the sound of steel striking bone as it passes through the flesh. It may be hard to explain but Rick knew how it felt because he had been stabbed before! Maybe that was the reason he loathed the Mexican so much! Frankie liked the knife and the knife brought a fear to Rick that he could not explain. Rick picked up the saddle and joined the rest of the men at the fire. He sat on the saddle as he reached for the coffee pot. Rick took his eyes off Frankie for only a second but that was all it took, Frankie was tired of waiting, he would have slit Rick's throat last night if it had not been for the stupid sticks around his bed role. He knew he could not have snuck up on him with the homemade alarm and would have gotten shot for his trouble if he had; this was the last morning he would have to put up with the man he hated so much! Frankie sat at the fire on Rick's left side, he held the knife in his right hand hidden behind the left arm, within seconds Rick would be dead! Rick had no third sense and no premonition of danger. As he sat on the saddle, it twisted and he fell to the right, Frankie swung the knife backhand towards Rick's throat as his butt touched the saddle. That little twist of the saddle may have saved Rick's life. It may be hard to explain how the bite of a knife feels but Rick knew and he felt it again as the knife in Frankie hand sliced through the flesh of his shoulder, separating flesh and muscle. He heard the sound of steel striking bone and felt the grinding of the blade. Rick was falling and he kept falling even as the blade missed it mark. Frankie was on his feet coming towards the man as Rick landed. There was no time to draw the pistol at his side so Rick did the only thing he could do he cocked the pistol and lifted his leg and fired through the holster! The bottom of the holster exploded as the shell flew out of the end. The bullet traveled along Rick's leg and struck Frankie in the center of the stomach, just inches above the belly. The Mexican looked like a rag doll as the bullet struck the back bone shattering the nerves and transforming him into a cripple. Frankie lay on the ground looking up as Rick stood. Never in his wildest dreams did Frankie think this could happen to him! Frankie watched as Rick held the weapon in his hand and pointed at the men by the fire. "I will kill anyone that moves!" he screamed as blood ran down his arm and chest. Rick backed towards the horses keeping his eyes on the men. They were men like Frankie and they were his friends, to turn his back to these men was sure death. Rick's horse was not saddled so he took the first one he came to with a saddle. It was a paint that looked like it could run and as soon as Rick was in the saddle he put the spurs to the animal trying to put as much distance between him and the men he hated. The wound was deep and blood flowed as he rode but Rick knew if he did not get help soon he would bleed to death. The only help he could think of was the very men he and the others had come to kill! One of the men at the fire walked over to Frankie, he even bent down and looked at the wound, "Mi amigo," he said, "You're in a bad way!" Frankie never saw the man remove the revolver but he heard the clicking of the hammer as it was cocked, it was the last thing he would ever hear, he never heard the sound of the shot as the shell passed through his skull! Yes these men were like Frankie and this is what he would have done.

Skip MacCland sat behind the desk in his office, "Those stupid deputies would not let Larry out of jail for love or money." He said cursing. He had tried bail but they would have none of it, they were going to hold the prisoner until a higher authority showed up and they did not care if it was the Marshal or the judge as long as they did not have to take responsibility. There was no way the Marshal would let him out of jail without a court order, it was up to Skip to make sure Larry was released. Skip did not care if Larry had killed two men in some other state, he did not care if he had killed Don Malloy in the middle of the Crooked Horn restaurant and he did not care if he had killed a hundred men, in fact the more the merrier, it just meant he was good at his job and right now Skip wanted Larry out of jail even if it was for a day, and hour or a minute, as long as he had time to kill the man that had ridden the black into town! Skip called to four of the men standing outside his office. They were a sorry looking lot for cowboys; they looked more like the kind of men who would hang around the bars at night rolling drunks and winos for the change in their pockets. Skip had plans to take over the whole valley but with men like these on the payroll it was not going to be easy to do. As the ranch grew he would have to replace them with better men but for now they would have to do. The judge will be coming within the next day or so and I want you men to watch the roads for him and stop him and bring him here. The man who brings him to me will get a hundred dollar bonus.

Skip watched the men leave, they were scum but they were the kind of scum he needed. For a hundred dollars they would bring him their own mothers! Skip knew the judge would be standing before him within the next few days.

K.C. poured the last of his coffee into the fire and began to kick dirt over the coals when he saw the rider coming across the flats; he was riding straight for the herd. No one was supposed to know they were there and this upset K.C. The man was not riding fast and hard like a man who was about to attack, in fact he was riding slow and leaning over his saddle like something was wrong. K.C. drew the rifle from the scabbard and waited as the rider came closer. K.C. was not stupid he knew this could be a trick to draw him out into the open and he knew he was hidden by the depth of the draw and he planned on having the first shot. As he set the sight of the rifle on the man's chest and began to squeeze the trigger he saw the blood on the man's shirt. This was no trick, even from that distance he could see the open gash and the flow of blood running down the man's arm falling to the ground below his horse. Rick knew he was close to the rustler's camp, if he could find it he had a chance of survival. They were not the kind of men he had been riding with, these cowboys might be quick with a trigger but they were not murderers. They were young and reckless but they had courage and strength. They would face a man straight on, man to man or gun to gun; he knew they would not send someone else to do their dirty work; they were not the kind to stab a man in the back. If he could find their camp he would get help. At one time Rick had been a strong independent person needing nothing and no one but that had been when he was young and strong himself but now he felt like a tired broken down old man. It was to his shame he found himself seeking help from the very people he had been sent to kill!

As he drew nearer and lifted his head K.C. realized he knew the man, the rider was one of the men that had held a gun on him as Mr. Malloy placed the rope around his neck. The thought of the rope around his neck sent a cold rage through him. If ever a man was tempted to shoot a helpless human being it was then, even as his finger tightened on the trigger he could feel the ruff cords of the rope as it was being twisted around his throat! "You know that would be murder." He knew the voice that came from behind him and he knew it was the truth. Lowering the rifle K.C. turned to look at Parker, "I know," he said, "But it was tempting." Parker shook his head, "Well, are you going to call him in or are you going to kill him?" K.C. lowered the rifle, "Hey Rick, this way!" he yelled. Rick figured he had nothing to lose as he rode the paint towards the speaker, the worst they could do was kill him and without help he would die anyway! "Climb down and let's have a look at that," Parker said pointing at the cut along Rick's chest and arm. As Rick leaned forward and swung his leg over the saddle horn a wave of nausea hit and he had to hang on as he slid off the horse. His legs felt like rubber as they tried to buckle under his weight. Rick mustered up all the strength he had to stand straight, if he was going to die he wanted to die as the man he had once been. For a few seconds he managed to stand straight and tall then his legs went out from under him. K.C. and Parker watched as he fell. "What are we going to do about him?"

Parker wanted to know. K.C. held his hands to his neck remembering the feel of the rope. "We're going to try to patch him up!" "Go through his saddle bags and see if he has anything to drink, he's going to need it when we put the stitches in him." Parker kicked the sand and dirt off the campfire and added a few branches. Digging a needle out of his saddle bag he laid it in the fire and after it turned crimson red he took a stick placed it on the center of the needle and pushed down bending the needle in a 'C' shape, "This will have to do," Parker said as he raked it from the fire. They found a bottle of whisky in the stolen saddle bags and held Rick up long enough to pour some of the liquid down his throat, it was a cheap brand of whisky and it nearly gagged him as the rot gut hit his stomach. Rick managed to focus his eyes as the taste of the bottled fire pulled him back to consciousness as K.C. poured the alcohol into the open wound. Rick set up and began to scream, "What are you trying to do kill me?" he yelled as he felt the burn of the alcohol in the wound. This man had tried to hang him and now he was complaining about the treatment he was receiving! K.C. shoved him back onto the ground, "This won't hurt near as much as the stitches," he said shoving the needle into the wound. Rick passed out from the lack of blood and the pain of the needle being shoved into his body. "What are we going to do with him now?" Parker wanted to know as they looked down at the now unconscious man. "Mary and a couple of her friends, Stephanie and Connie are supposed to meet us this side of the border with some grub, and if they are there they will be riding a buck board so send Colton to find them and the rest of you keep pushing the cattle south, I'll stay with him until they get here. They can take him back to town with them, maybe a doctor there can do a better job than I did. I'll catch up with the herd after we get him loaded." Parker took off to find Colton and the herd as the men of the Rocking 'R' ranch brought the judge before Skip MacCland.

"How much does it pay?" he asked looking at the man behind the desk. Judge hicks had heard the men talking on the way back to the ranch and if Skip MacCland was willing to pay one hundred dollars to this kind of scum to bring him to the ranch then surely he was worth a lot more. Skip counted out a thousand dollars in hundred dollar bills and laid it on the desk, counting the bribes and kick backs, that was more money than the judge would make in a year. "What do you want done?" Hicks asked as he picked up the money. "Not much," Skip began, "All you have to do is let Larry Cheatham out of jail." "A thousand dollars was a lot of money as far as the judge was concerned and it was more than enough, "When do you want him out?" "As soon as possible!" Skip said, "He has a lot of work to do." Skip wanted the gunman on the black horse killed and the three cowboys killed or driven out of town, all his plans hung on the gunman in the cell. As Judge Hicks left his office Skip leaned back in his chair, he was the only man in the country that knew who the rider on the black horse was. True they had only met for an instant but that instant had been long enough to burn the man's image into his memory forever! Years ago, Skip had looked through a pair of field glasses to see a small insignificant man wearing Captain's bars leading a troop of Calvary soldiers and the solid blue colors of the uniform made the man look even smaller. Some of the men were already wounded, wearing blood red bandages. It would be an easy victory for the confederate soldiers under his command. His men were scattered out in the woods waiting for the cavalry to pass by then they would take the Captain and his men from the rear cutting them to pieces before they knew what happened. It was a perfect plan and it had been calculated with a precision that comes only with the experience of men who had done this kind of thing before. Hiding behind trees and brush his men cut loose with the rifles dropping the union soldiers from their saddles with the very first volley as their shells found their marks. Everything was going fine until the Captain rode back, he had looked like a man possessed as he drew the rifle out of the scabbard. Skips men had begun to flee even before the fire power of the captain's rifle was emptied! Man after man fell trying to escape the deadly shells as they found their marks. Skip had never feared man or beast until that moment. The Captain slid the rifle back into its scabbard and pulled the pistols from holsters around his hips, fire and flame erupted as he sighted on the men now too terrified to lift their heads. Skip lay on his belly watching as his men were cut down, somehow he knew one day the wild man with the flaming pistols would take his life. The Captain stopped at the rear of the column looking like a protecting angel or a rampaging demon straight from the pits of hell, pistols in both hands protecting the remains of his fallen men. The thought of the battle put a fear into Skip that he had not known since the war. For the second time in his life he knew real fear. The judge did not know it but Skip would have paid ten times that much to see Larry freed!

"Hey, are you going to have breakfast or are you going to sleep all day?" Joe asked as he kicked the Marshal's foot. Jim sat up to the smell of the beans. Sometime during the night Joe had put a hand full of beans into the pot of water he had put on that night, probably after he snuck out to practice with the pistols Jim deduced. Joe put half the beans on a metal plate and handed the pot to the Marshal. Pushing the sand from over the smoldering ashes Joe brought out two potatoes, "You got the most beans," he said, "so you get the smallest potato!" and with that Joe handed him the rest of breakfast. Jim broke up the potato and put it in with the beans, added some of the salt Sherlene had packed and began to eat, it was a lot better than the fried bacon and the hard tack biscuits they had been eating! "When you're finished with the pot we'll put on some coffee," Joe said as he dug into his plate of the cowboy breakfast. "Where do you think they will make their play?" Jim asked still digging into the plate of beans. "One the other side of the hill is a draw that widens out, K.C. and his bunch will be forced into the open if they stick with the route their taking that is the way I think they will come. The men following them will set up on the side of the draw and ambush them as they come into the open." "What are we going to do about it?" Jim asked, "We'll wait upon the top of the hill and when they start to cut loose on the kids and the herd we'll get them. From the top of the hill to the bottom of the draw must be four hundred yards," Jim said, "I don't think I can hit a horse at that distance much less a man, besides we have to give them a chance to give up it's the law!" "You're not the law in Mexico!" Joe stated, "as far as their concerned their nothing but a lynch mob and you know it!" "We can't shoot them in cold blood, it's not right!" Jim was beginning to wonder if he had brought the right man after all! "Their planning on murdering four men and a girl, and if we don't stop them here they will do it someplace else when we're not around, do you want that on your conscience?" Joe barked back. "Besides, you're the one who said you could not hit the broadside of a barn if you were standing in it! Chances are you won't hit anything or anyone! All you have to do is make noise and leave the shooting to me!"

Judge Hicks left the Rocking 'R' a thousand dollars richer and like Skip MacCland, he did not care if the man in the jail cell had killed one man or a hundred as long as he was getting paid! It made no difference to him, he was tired of being a servant to the people and wanted more out of life than the position of judge and with this kind of money he could run for an office of some kind, maybe become Mayor of one of the many towns he passed through. With some backing he might even run for Governor! Anything was better than riding around the country in a buckboard dealing with the kind of derelicts he had to put up with everyday. If he did this favor for the owner of the Rocking 'R' ranch maybe he would be the one to back him in the future. It was with these thoughts Judge Hicks checked into the hotel across the street from the Crooked Horn. He was going to take a bath and shave before going to the Marshal's office to free the prisoner, he wanted to look respectable!

Rick was surprised to still be alive as K.C. and the women loaded him into the buckboard. "I thought I would have bled to death by now!" Rick said as he was laid in the bottom of the wagon. "Not hardly," K.C. said, "these three ladies will get some steak and beans in you and you'll be as good as new in a few weeks!" Rick owed his life to these people, "listen," he said, "the Rocking 'R' men have been trailing you, they know you're traveling the draws. Ten miles on the other side of the border they plan on jumping you and driving the cattle off. They want it to look like Mexican banditos had killed you all off and that way no one could put the blame on them." "Who is behind it?" Mary asked. "Both ranches, the Rocking 'R' and the Malloy outfit want to see all of you dead!" "Why?" Connie asked, "We've done nothing to them?" "Skip MacCland made plans to buy the Malloy ranch from Nicole's uncle. Her uncle has been losing a lot of money at the gambling tables and it's the only way he could pay back the debt he owed. As far as Skip Malloy was concerned, he was going to get the ranch dirt cheap since most of the debt was to him and he wants to be the only rancher in the valley. He brought Cheatham in to get rid of the three cowboys holding on to the northeast corner of the valley, only his plans changed when he saw the cowboy ride in on that black stallion and all of a sudden he decided to have him killed first!" "You mean the broken down drifter riding the bunk next to me in the jail?" K.C. said, "What's so important about him?" Rick shook his head, "don't know, the boss is scared to death of him for some reason!" "That doesn't sound like MacCland!" Stephanie put in. "No it don't, Rick said, but it's the truth!" "Mary, you Stephanie, and Connie get him out of here and try to find him a doctor," K.C. instructed the women, "I've got to get to the herd and get them out of the draw and warn Eric and the rest that their riding into a trap!" "Colton and Parker should have caught up with the herd by now, they know about Rick so maybe they've got everybody on their guard!"

Judge Hicks could not believe it, those stupid deputy's had tried to give him a hard time, they did not want to release the prisoner, said they "wanted to wait for an answer to a telegraph they had sent before they released him." Well he showed them, told them the shooting was a clear case of self defense and they had no right to hold him any longer and if they did not do as the court instructed he would have them jailed for contempt! They didn't even want to give the man his gun back. Judge Hicks planned to have a talk with the Marshal when he got back! If he could not find men who would obey a court order he would have them all replaced!

Larry walked out of the jail a free man and even if the telegraph came back showing he was a wanted man the Judge had told him he would resend the order and if he had to he was willing to write him a full pardon! He didn't know if it was legal or not but neither would anyone else and he would still be free to kill the drifter, pick up his money and head back to Mexico. After that life was a gamble and he was a pretty good gambler. Larry went to the hotel and checked into his room. His bed role was still lying in the corner and if MacCland was willing to pay off a judge to get him out of jail, that meant the drifter was better with a gun. Ship did not look like the kind of man that had to have someone else do his killing. Larry untied the bed role and spread it out. Here was the weapon he was good with, not the little hide out gun strapped to his shoulder. This was a full scale forty-four in a quick draw holster! After ejecting the shells into his hand Larry began taking the pistol apart, he was going to check and oil every piece. It was not his nature to go unprepared into a gunfight. He wanted to make sure his pistol did not jam or misfire when he needed it most! He oiled the holster and slid the pistol gently into the pre-molded leather. Strapping the gun belt on he began to practice his draw, a split second meant the difference between life and death to a gunfighter. From this point on there would be no more booze and no more women. He had to hone his senses to a razors edge.

As long as the cattle were in the draw, K.C. knew the live of his brother and cousins were in danger so he pushed his horse to the limit, trying to catch up to them! Rick had told him how the fight with Frankie Vasquez had started and how many men were left. Without their leader they might have changed their plans, they could even now be attacking his family! He caught up to the herd and the rest of the men as they crossed the border and for the first time since he broke jail he knew for certain that men followed him and his crew with the intent to murder each and every one of them! Now was the time to decide if they wanted to scatter the herd or try to make it to the cattle buyers further into the Mexican territory. They needed the money to fight for the ranch. Nicole would soon be old enough to legally take control of the ranch but was it worth risking their lives? Nicole and the men sat watching the herd as it moved slowly south, within hours they were going to know if the risk was worth it as they had decided to keep the herd. They were going to be coming out of the draws into the open and if the men of the Rocking 'R' and Malloy ranch knew where they were it made no sense trying to hide now! K.C. and his men were going to change direction and head into the valley, at least that way they might be able to see the men coming before they spotted them. Colton would ride scout circling the herd on the lookout for Mexican bandits or the ambush that was sure to come and with any luck they would survive the next few days! The rest of the men would drive the cattle with their rifles at the ready, watching every movement.

All that day Joe and the Marshal sat on top of the hill waiting for the ambush that was never going to come not knowing that the cattle and the men had turned further west avoiding the draws altogether. As night fell

Joe built a fire behind the cover of the mountain, something was wrong, he could feel it in his bones, the cattle and the men should have been there by now! In the morning he planned on taking a ride across the border and see if he could find them. Somewhere there was going to be a massacre and he planned on being there to stop it! As the sun began to rise, Joe was up and finishing a cup of coffee. After saddling the black he headed north looking for the trail of the cattle. Joe found the trail where a small herd of cattle crossed the border. The tracks were fresh and the center of the dung was still warm. This had to be the men he wanted to catch. Joe swung the reins of the black and headed southwest in the direction the herd had taken and with any luck he would catch them within the hour!

K.C. and the rest of his outfit had pushed the cattle most of the night, seeing mostly by the light of the moon, trying desperately to outrun the men behind them. They had broke camp early, eating biscuits and bacon and now they were trying to get as far ahead of the gunmen as they could and with any luck they might even lose them with the change in directions and starting to move the cattle even before the sun was up. Joe was already gone when Jim woke up, walking to the fire he poured himself a cup of coffee wondering where the temporary deputy had went. It never occurred to him that Joe had gone hunting five armed men by himself!

Eric heard the bullet whiz past his face and then the sound of the rifle shot. Colton spurred his horse to a dead run at the sound of the shot. The men firing lay in a ditch two hundred yards to the east where smoke from the barrels of the rifles gave their position away. The first volley of shots had been fired in hast missing the mark by inches. It was the young rustlers turn to open fire but it was a hard shot with the lynch mob hiding in the ditch. The young cowboys had been lucky during the first part of the attack; their luck might not hold if they tried to get to their horses now! To charge was to run into the face of the enemy and the hail of lead that would be heading their way. K.C. and his men lay flat in the dirt unable to move as the enemy sought the flesh of their bodies with the lead of their bullets. The Marshal may have been a heavy sleeper but even he could hear the sounds of gun fire coming from across the valley! This was not the spot Joe had picked for the ambush to take place. Jim threw his saddle on the roan, it was going to take a while for him to get there and with any luck maybe some of the young rustler's might still be alive! Joe topped the rise as he heard the sound of gun fire erupt. The loud bark of the rifles drowned out the sound of the pistols as the Malloy outfit fired time and time again at the men lying helpless on the ground. At one time this was the kind of battles Joe had lived for and turning the black into the ditch Joe dug his heels into the horse's sides so when they came around the bend they would be face to face with the men in the ditch. The rifle would have too long a barrel for the close quarter fighting and it would take too long to cock after each shot. Joe left the rifle in the scabbard and drew the pistols at his sides. Jim raced to the site of the battle trying to get there before everyone of those fool hardy kids was killed. If he got there in time maybe he could stop the slaughter! Jim topped the ridge in time to see the last of the battle. Jim sat on the back of his horse and watched as Joe and the black charged down the ditch. Joe held a pistol in both hands and even from that distance Jim could see the look of an avenging angel or the look of a demon straight from the pits of hell on Joe's face! This was the look on the man's face that had put a fear into Skip MacCland that had haunted him to this day and this was the reason Skip had hired a gunman instead of facing the man himself. The men of the Rocking 'R' heard the sounds of the blacks hooves coming at them and turned to fire but it was too late, the pistols in Joe's hands began to spit fire. These men had come to ambush and kill they never thought that a wild man was going to becoming at them with guns a blazing! They tried to face the man and meet him head on and as they fired it was in haste and the shells were missing man and beast alike! Joe's pistols spoke loud and clear and the shells went true, the three men went down in a hail of lead. Joe sat in the saddle of the black, pistols cocked with a wild look in his eyes searching for the other two men. "That's enough!" K.C. yelled to the man who had stayed in the cell next to him and waving his arms trying to calm the man down. Jim put the spurs to the roan and started down the hill, there had been enough killing, and maybe he could stop the madness! "That's all of them!" K.C. yelled. "Frankie stabbed Rick back at their camp, he showed up here yesterday and we sent him back to town on a buckboard with some people we know. Rick wound up gut shooting Vasquez and if he ain't with them, then I guess he is back at these guys camp somewhere." Joe lowered the pistols and looked at the small group of rustlers, "Dang boys, you almost got yourselves killed!" he said as he turned the black to face the Marshal, "Where you been?" Joe had transformed himself back into the worn out looking saddle tramp and no one would have guessed that he had just killed three men! "Marshal, you're out of your jurisdiction, you got no authority down here!" K.C. said watching to see if the Marshal was going to try to arrest them for stealing the cattle and jail break. "Besides Nicole is going to own the place in a month and she said I could take the cattle." "Let me guess," Jim said, "you're going to sell the cattle, hire some gunmen and take the ranch back, is that about right?" "That was the plan," K.C. admitted. "In that case you're going to need this," Jim said digging into the saddle bags on the back of his horse. K.C. watched as the Marshal pulled a fancy quick draw gun belt with a silver star from the bag and a pearl handled pistol from the other and handed it to the young cowboy. "Don't shoot yourself with it!" Jim said as he handed him the bullets. "You mean you did not come down here to arrest us?" Eric asked in amazement. "Never planned on it!" Jim said, "Just wanted to make sure you made it alright. If I was going to arrest you I would have done it on the other side of the border!" "Will you do me a favor boys?" the Marshal asked. "Sure," one of the young men answered, "what can we do for you?" He wanted to know. "Bury these guys and bury them deep. I don't want the dogs to dig them up or the Federalies to find them. It would not look good for the states if Mexico found out that we were having our own private wars on their lands!" "Don't worry," Eric said, "We'll bury them half way to China," and then laughed at his own joke. Jim rode over and picked up the horses that had been used by the dead men. Two of the horses carried the Rocking 'R' brand and the other was from the Malloy ranch. "Now if you will excuse me my friend and I have a long ways to go." Jim turned his horse and headed north following the tracks of the horses back to dead men's camp. Somewhere back there was a gut shot man maybe they could find him before he died! Joe looked at the young men, "you boys be careful in Mexico, this place can be rough!" he said as he turned the black and followed the Marshal north back to the states and the brown eyed woman he found himself dreaming of. For the first time in years Joe had had something on his mind other than the speed of his hands or the battles of a war long past.

Finding the camp was not hard; the men did not think anybody was going to be following them and had not bothered to cover their tracks. The two men were greeted by the smell of dead, rotting flesh as they neared the camp. "Darn, they did not even bother burying the man!" Joe said as they looked down at the body. Frankie had been gut shot alright but the hole through his head told the rest of the story. "I guess they did not want to waste time on a corpse." Jim said disgustedly as he swung down from the horse, "hope you've got a shovel because we're going to have to bury him!" Joe shook his head, "No, but I figure there is shovel on one of their horses, after all they planned on burying the bodies of the others!" Jim dug through the saddle bags and came up with two small shovels and handing one to Joe he began to look for a place to bury the body. "We'll camp someplace else tonight!" he said as he tamped the last of the dirt on the grave. "That's alright with me!" Joe said, "I've seen and smelled enough dead bodies lately, I don't plan on sleeping with it!" The sun was beginning to set as they saddled up and left the camp of the dead!

Jim rode the roan up to large west Texas pond three or four miles north of the Mexican border and dismounted, "Did you ever think of being a peace officer Joe, the pays pretty good and the hours are short." Jim was in a talking mood as he searched for a fishhook and some line. "Now that the battle was over he planned to relax and kicking at the cow pies nearby he found some marble bugs and placed them on a hook. The Marshal pulled his boots off and waded into the water. The perch weren't big but they would cover the pan. Joe started the fire as Jim waded around in the pond, both men needed to relax and this was their way of doing it. Joe placed some bacon in a pan and placed it on the red coals. Jim cleaned the fish, rolled them in flour and placed them in the bacon grease and soon the aroma of fried fish and bacon filled the air. If a man was going to camp this was the way to do it. Without a care in the world Jim unrolled his bedroll, laid down and fell asleep. Jim awoke to the sounds of movement and the smell of coffee. Joe was already up and saddling the black, "What's the hurry?" he asked. Joe shrugged his shoulders, "Just want to get back to town, I guess I'm tired of living in the desert!" Jim had the feeling it was not town he was thinking of, maybe Joe was missing Marilyn. The waitress had taken quite a liking to the quiet drifter and maybe the feeling was mutual after all. Jim packed up the rest of the camp supplies and saddled his horse in thoughtful silence. First he had to take the horses back to the Rocking 'R' ranch, that meant facing Skip MacCland and the rest of the men at the ranch and then he had to tell Malloy two of his men were dead and that he didn't know where his horses were and he had to tell both of them that their plans had failed and the rustlers were still alive and in Mexico. The Marshal didn't know Don Malloy was already dead or that Skip MacCland had quit worrying about the rustlers, the cattle or the Malloy ranch. He didn't care if his men came back from Mexico dead or alive it made no difference to him at all, all he wanted was to see the rider on the black horse dead! Years earlier lying on his belly watching as his men were being cut down, Skip had a premonition of the duel between him and the gunman and ever since the man had ridden into town, the feeling had followed him like a ghost haunting him, even in his sleep! At night Skip dreamed of the battle fought long ago only this time he did not lie on his belly in fear this time he dreamed of standing and facing the man with his guns blazing but the dream was always the same, even as he fired he saw the bullet coming at him in slow motion seeking his heart! Skip would wake up just as the bullet penetrated the flesh. He would awake grabbing at his chest fearing the death that was about to come! The man had to die so Skip could live!

Joe and the Marshal topped the hill overlooking the town. The red roof of Nita's cat house was the first thing he noticed with its wrap around veranda and balcony facing the main street. "One day I'm going to have to do something about that," he thought. The rest of the town looked like a lot of other western towns with a barn and stable which the blacksmith shop run by a man named Garry was next to it. The town had a two story hotel own by a very nice couple named Damon and Mary and general store that Ashley owned and of course there was the Crooked Horn Restaurant and bar along with the jail, a school house that served as a church on Sundays, the bank and a telegraph office. There were several houses scattered out around town, they belonged to the people that mostly worked in town. From the hill top Jim could even see the smoke coming from the chimney of the Lazy Bar ranch. It belonged to the three hellions, Roy, Bobby and Mike. Just the thought of the three young men made him smile. He didn't want anyone to know but he liked the men. He didn't know where they had come from but he knew all three of men had hired on as drovers for a large cattle company. Two years earlier they had driven several thousand head of cattle over the Chisholm Trail. Unlike the rest of the drovers, when the men got to Kansas instead of drinking up their wages or losing them at the card tables they headed to Texas looking for a ranch of their own. Why they had settled here in a quiet little town was beyond Jim's reasoning, they were wild and rowdy with a little bit of funny thrown in and it made no sense that they would pick this town as their home. Jim was lost in his thoughts and was jarred back to reality as Joe spoke. "If I was you," Joe said "I'd let them horses go, they can find their own way home and it would save you a lot of riding. It might deep you from getting your head blown off by some friend of theirs looking for revenge!" Jim didn't think these men had been the kind of men to have friends but it would save him a lot of riding! Letting the horses go he fired a shot at their hooves, spooking them into a run, "They will be home pretty quick," he said as they started off the hill.

Sherlene and Marilyn watched as the two men started towards town and at the sight of them they both became excited, "You put on some coffee," Marilyn said as she headed for the mirror. Still standing behind the bar she began taking the pins from her hair and letting it fall to her shoulders, "For once I'm glad Paul is a slow mover," she said pulling a brush through her hair, "I would hate to do this from a reflection on a skillet!" "Especially Eloise's skillet!" Sherlene put in as both women began to giggle at the remark. Marilyn went into the kitchen and dabbed some vanilla on her wrists and at the nape of her neck, "he won't get that close!" Sherlene said as she watched her apply the homemade perfume. "You never can tell!" Marilyn commented smiling at the thought of the man being that close to her. Like Skip MacCland she had dreamed of the man since the day he had ridden into town but her dreams weren't of battles and wars, her dreams were of a family and a home and one day she planned on having both of them and this was the man she had been waiting for! Sherlene and Marilyn watched as Joe and the Marshal brought their horses to a stop in front of the marshal's office and climbed off the mounts. Both men looked tired and worn out and they were stiff from the long ride and stretched as their feet hit the ground. The black still looked half wild but had gotten used to the roan and let the animal stand close to him. Joe and the Marshal tied the horses to the wooden rail and went inside. Both men wanted to clean up before heading to the Crooked Horn to see the women they were in love with. Jim stoked the coals in the stove and got a fire going as Joe placed a pan of water over the burners. Schon watched as the two tried to make themselves presentable, "Had a little excitement around here while you were gone." He informed the two men as they took out the straight razors and began to shave. "How is that?" Jim asked between strokes of the blade. "Fellow named Larry Cheatham killed Don Malloy at the Crooked Horn!" Jim stopped shaving, "Anyone else hurt?" he asked. Jim was worried about the women. "No just Malloy, he was killed over a card game, said the other guy cheated and went for his gun and got shot for the trouble." "I didn't think Malloy would try a gun!" Jim said "the man was a worse shot than I am!" "Maybe he would not have, Schon answered, but he thought the other fellow was unarmed but the gambler pulled a sneak gun from under his shoulder and blew a hole clear through him." "Where is the gambler now?" the Marshal wanted to know. "Well, me and Rog had him locked up and we tried to hold him until you returned. Ashley had told us he was wanted in Louisiana for murder. I sent some telegraphs but never got an answer but like I said, we tried to keep him in jail until we found out if he was still wanted or not but the judge told us if we did not let him go he would take our badges and hold us in contempt of court!" "Not sure if that is legal or not but I'm not going to worry about it right now, I'm pretty sure Sherlene and Marilyn are waiting for us the Crooked Horn. I'm tired and hungry, we've been eating out of a pot and drinking hobo coffee for days and I can't wait to see Sherlene and give her a big hug and wrap my teeth around a good meal and I'm pretty sure Joe would like to do the same thing only with a different woman," Jim emphasized the remark. "You think Joe wants to see his girlfriend?" Rog asked. Schon still thought of Joe as another drifter and laughed at the thought of Joe and the waitress being together, "You're kidding, right?" Schon asked. "No, I think Marilyn and Joe are kind of sweet on each other!" Jim teased as he headed out the door. "Last one to the Crooked Horn buys!" he said as he slammed the door behind him, he had discovered you had to take every advantage you can when dealing with Joe! Jim was right; both women had watched the men go into the Marshal's office and were waiting for them as they emerged. Marilyn was primping with her hair trying to make it perfect, she wanted to make more than a good impression, she wanted to be beautiful. "How do I look?" she asked her sister. "Well let me think, you look just like the cat that's about to jump on a mouse and he ain't got a chance!" "That's how I wanted to look!" Marilyn said, "I don't intend to give him a chance!" The smell of vanilla filled the room, "Alright," Jim said walking into the room, "Somebody's cooking a cake." Sherlene gave her husband a hug, "Shut up!" she whispered as she pulled him up close. "You mean you ain't cooking a cake, I'm disappointed after all you saw me a coming!" "Shut up!" she whispered again. Jim had been married long enough to know women used the vanilla as perfume and Marilyn was trying to entice Joe. Jim was going to have fun teasing her but Sherlene put a stop to his fun with a few quietly whispered words, "Keep it up and you will be sleeping alone!" She may or may not have meant it but Jim was taking no chances! "Yes, dear!" was all he had to say and those were the exact words Sherlene wanted to hear! All four of them sat down to a quiet meal as Paul carried boxes of booze out the front doors. "Where is he going?" Jim asked surprised that Paul would be leaving. "I bought him out!" Marilyn said with a sound of pride in her voice, "I now own three fourths of the restaurant! "Heck," Jim teased, "Get Eloise to eat some of her own cooking and you'll own the whole thing!" Eloise heard the remark and came out of the kitchen carrying a skillet, "One more crack," she said "and I'll slap you upside the head with this thing!" Marilyn remembered the remarks made by Bobby and Roy, she drew back in mock fear, "oh no not the beans!" she cried. Everyone at the table began to laugh at the expression on Eloise's face, "you keep it up and you'll be eating you own cooking!" she said as she headed back into the kitchen. "You call that a threat?" Jim wanted to know, "it sounds more like a blessing to me!" he said. After hearing that remark, Eloise turned and threw the skillet from halfway across the room, missing the Marshal by six feet, "you throw even worse than you cook!" Eloise had heard all of the comments she wanted and headed for the kitchen, "I meant to miss!" she said, "I would not want to get arrested for assault to an idiot!"

The crew of the Lazy Bar ranch came into the restaurant, well at least Roy and Mike came in, "We want a well smoked right hind quarter of a hog and two bags shoved full of hard tack biscuits and make sure it's the right hind quarter!" Mike ordered, "Were gonna be branding cattle on the south forty and we don't want to be stumbling around lopsided!" both men laughed at the homemade humor. "If you boys are gonna be branding won't you be needing Bobby?" Marilyn asked. "We sure will!" Mike put in "but ever since the new girl went to work at Nita's we've been having a hard time keeping him at the ranch! He runs off every five minutes! Talk about love sick, he's named six caves and a puppy Michelle!" "That would not be so bad except, the puppy was a male and two of the calves were bulls!" Roy and Mike sat down and had coffee while they waited for their order. These two loved to upset Marilyn and continued with their banter, "Talk about bad, the water that was used in this coffee must have come from the Mississippi River because it tastes like mud!" Mike laughed. "To heck with the mud," Roy said holding back a smile, "It smells like a catfish is hiding behind the coffee grounds in this cup!" "I'll get you a shovel!" Mike said, "We'll have that puppy for dinner!" "Alright, knock it off!" "Why does everyone give Eloise a hard time?" "Besides she's not the one who made the coffee!" "We know, Roy said, her's ain't nearly this bad!" "What did you do, they asked; try your hand at cookin? I'll bet Marilyn has never teased Eloise about her cookin, have you?" Mike wanted to know. The question floored her, how could she say anything when just minutes before she had been doing the same thing! Marilyn gave the boys her best imitation look of anger, "Keep it up and I'll have you both thrown out of here for good!" she warned knowing she would never do that!

Skip MacCland sat on the veranda of his home on the Rocking 'R' ranch sipping from a bottle of fine whisky, the sun was just beginning to set as he saw the rider approaching, it was Tim, one of the ranch hands and saddled horses followed the rider. The horses turned and headed to the barn as the rider approached the main house. "Brought some horses in, he stated, they were already saddled when we found them!" Skip did not have to be told who they had belonged to! He had seen the horses, they belonged to the men he had sent to gun down the rustlers on their way to Mexico, "He killed them all!" Skip said quietly. He had not meant to speak out loud; it was more of a statement to himself! "Who killed them all?" Tim wanted to know. Skip was brought out of a stress induced trance and without thinking Skip began to explain. "The Marshal is more farmer than lawman, he sure ain't no gunman! That bunch of young rustlers did not know they were riding into an ambush and even if they did I doubt if they could have beaten the men we sent after them, which leaves on person, the drifter, the man on the black horse!" Tim shook his head, "Ain't no way one person killed all five of them!" "Don't you bet on it!" Skip said and shut up. He didn't want the rest of the men to know he had met the drifter before. "I want you to put the horses in the barn then ride to town and bring me the man that killed Don Malloy, he's staying at the hotel in room fourteen, the one facing the street and if he ain't there he will probably be at Nita's! Don't come back to the ranch without him!" Tim went to the barn and took the saddles off two of the mounts and placed them in a stall, gave them some grain and took the saddle off his own horse and put it in a stall also. Tim mounted the third horse, "I don't think your owner is gonna mind!" he said and followed the road into town.

Jim stretched out his arm, "I'll be taking the badge now!" Joe took the badge from his shirt and handed it to the Marshal, "What now?" he asked. "I guess you'll be spending the night in the jail!" Joe stiffened, "I thought you were going to get that taken care of?" "I will, in the morning. I'm letting the deputies have the night off, besides I've kind of grown fond of you're company and the bunks at the jail are softer than the beds at the hotel! You won't have to pay for a nights lodging either!" Joe relaxed, "I'll go but I ain't gonna like it!" he complained. "Oh well, I'll teach you how to play cards," Jim said. Both men laughed, Jim could play cards no better than he could shoot. Joe took off his gun belt and hung it on the hook behind the Marshal's desk, "Hey, if I'm a prisoner again, I want Marilyn to bring me my breakfast!" Jim didn't think he was going to have a problem honoring the request. "I'll see what I can do!" he said as he hung his own gun belt up. "Get some sleep, I've gotta make rounds in a few hours.

The blast of a shotgun woke both men. Joe sat up and began to stomp his boots on as he heard the tumbling of the lock. Jim stood at the door locking him in. "Just keeping you out of trouble," he said as he ran for his own boots. Another blast of the shotgun echoed through the jail, vibrating the walls. Joe sat and watched as Jim went out the door. Joe did not know it but he had gotten to where he liked the Marshal. Joe sat in the dark of the night and waited for the return of the marshal and he was not surprised as the men came through the door, it was Roy and Mike. The marshal followed carrying a ten gage shotgun. "Alright, in the cell you two!" he said leaning the shotgun against the wall. Both men walked into the cell and Jim locked the door. "Joe I've got to make rounds and these guys woke half the town up and some of them are gonna be screaming mad, if I unlock you cell will you see if you can keep them quiet?" "For a prisoner you sure keep me working!" Joe said. "That's because you're better at it than me," Jim replied as he rushed out. "Heck, I should be getting a paycheck!" Joe complained as he sat behind the Marshal's desk. Roy had walked over to the bunk, laid down and passed out and Joe wanted to know why Jim had brought the men in before Mike did likewise and passed out too! "Why did the Marshal bring you boys in anyway?" he asked Mike. "I thought you were going to be branding by now!" "We was gonna be brandin but as soon as we got home the dog got a hold of the hog and headed under the house and by the time we got it back weren't nothin left but bone. We came back to town to get another, one thing led to another and next thing I knowed we were drunk and being arrested!" "Why were you shooting?" Joe wanted to know. Mike looked kind of embarrassed, "Roy bet me five dollars that he could rick-a-shay a bullet off one of those biscuits." "Well, did he manage to do it?" Joe asked. "Heck no!" Mike said, "He was too drunk, he couldn't hit the darn thing with a shotgun from ten feet!" "Well I'll see you in the morning," Joe said letting the cowboy know it was time to pass out. Mike walked over to a bunk, lay down and obliged the part time marshal. Joe sat in the chair with his feet kicked up on the desk, "I could get used to this," he thought as he nodded off dreaming of tomorrow and soft brown eyes.

Tim heard the blasts of the shotgun as he rode into town but it was no skin off my nose if some drunks blow off steam," he thought as he swung down in front of Paul's new bar. It really was not much of a bar just a large tent with boards thrown over a couple of beer kegs. Card tables were scattered about and the chairs were pieces of firewood stood on end. The beer was going to be hot until he got a ice house dug but Tim didn't care, like most of the cowboys, he preferred whisky. The real bar was being built next door; stakes were already in place showing the outline of the new building. "It wouldn't be long before Paul had the bar he dreamed of," Tim thought as he ordered a whisky at the make shift counter. "Paul, have you seen the fellow that gunned down Malloy?" Paul stopped wiping at the planks of the bar, "He moved out of the hotel, some of the drover said they been hearing a lot of gun fire four or five miles north of town. I kind of figured it's him getting ready for something." Thanks!" Tim said, "If he comes in tell him I'm waiting for him at the hotel, Skip want s to see him as soon as possible!" Paul finished wiping the planks as Tem left. Paul never figured himself a smart man but even he knew when Skip MacCland sent for a gunman trouble was coming. "I best warn the Marshal!" Paul thought as he took a shot of his own whisky. Paul was waiting for him as Jim walked through the flaps of the tent that served as a door, "looks like you got trouble!" Paul placed a hot beer on the bar as he spoke. "Skip MacCland sent Tim into town looking for that Cheatham fellow. I never figured I'd live to see the day when MacCland don't want to do his own killin! I figure he either brought the gunman here or he is planning on hiring him to do some killin for him!" Jim was beginning to wish he really was a Marshal, not just some farmer voted into the job. Maybe then he would know what to do about men like Cheatham and MacCland. This had been a nice quiet little town when he applied for the job but now things were getting out of hand and he knew he didn't have the experience to keep a lid on things that were about to happen!

Like most cowboys Tim hated to get out of a soft bed but the boss was in a hurry so he climbed out of bed early that morning to find the gunman. After saddling his horse he rode north and had only ridden a little better than two miles when he heard the sound of gunfire. "That has got to be Cheatham," he thought as he followed the sounds of the shots. Riding to the top of the hill he could see a man down below. There was a fence post in the ground ten feet in front of him. Tim could see the holes in the wood and as he watched the man drew and fired, fanning the pistol with his left hand. Pieces of wood flew from the post as the soft lead found their mark. Up until that point Tim had thought Skip was the fastest man with a gun he had ever seen but the gunman was quicker! He thought as he rode towards the man. Tim had no way of knowing that Skip had quit riding the range the day the drifter had shown up, he spent his days behind the main house practicing his draw. His pistol was drawn from the holster in one smooth motion, it was quick and it was the fastest it had ever been in his life. He was just as fast as Cheatham and just as accurate! Tim didn't bother getting down from the horse, "Boss wants to see you!" he said watching the man's expression. Tim was afraid of the man and didn't want to make him mad but the gunman was not upset, he knew MacCland would be sending for him, after all he had not killed the drifter yet! He wanted to know all he could about Skip and the drifter both but Tim was not much help. He tried all the way while following Tim to the Rocking 'R' ranch but the only thing he knew for certain was MacCland didn't want to face the drifter with a gun.

Skip sat on the veranda sipping whisky and watching the men as they rode up. Larry saw the bottle even before he dismounted from the horse. "Liquid courage!" he thought to himself, "This guy has got the jitters real bad!" That was good for Larry he could hold him up for even more money. Skip wanted to know why the man was not dead yet but he acted as if he was in no hurry, he met Larry half way down the steps, "How have you been?" he asked with his hand stretched out to the gunman. Larry could see the fear in Skip's eyes, this job was going to pay more than the five hundred dollars he had already received, "Fine," he said knowing the real question Skip wanted answered. MacCland couldn't contain himself any longer,

"When are you going to kill him!" he sneered not caring if the gunman knew he feared the man he had been paid to get rid of. "That depends, Larry said, on how much it pays!" Skip didn't like the attitude of the man, "I already paid you!" he hissed. Larry shook his head, "That was to kill a nobody and I don't think the drifter is a nobody or you would have killed him you're self!" "How much to kill the drifter?" Skip asked his patients running low. He was at the breaking point and was unable to endure the waiting any longer. "A thousand now and another thousand after the job is done!" Larry said calmly, he knew MacCland would pay whatever he asked. Skip took out another five hundred dollars, "I've already paid you five, this will square us up for now but I still want to know when will the job be done?" "Tomorrow," Larry said, "after lunch!" "Then you will spend the night here!" Skip demanded. "Tomorrow I'm riding into town with you!" "What's the matter, don't you trust me?" Larry said. "No," Skip answered; before I pay you I have to see the man dead and I want to see him die with my own eyes!" Larry didn't care if his employer wanted to watch the death of an enemy as long as he got paid. "Suit yourself," he said and walked past Skip into the main house as if he owned it!

"Alright you two, get up and get out!" the Marshal growled. Roy and Mike climbed from their bunks about the time Jim through a mop in the cell, "If you made the mess you clean it up!" he said. Joe was already up and shaving, "I worked last night so you're buying breakfast!" "I ain't bought a meal since I took this job," Jim stated but since it's a special occasion I guess I will!" Joe stopped shaving, "What special occasion is that?" he asked. "Why you get to see your girlfriend of course, what else would it be?" It was close to noon as the two men headed for the Crooked Horn, Sherlene and Marilyn had been watching for the marshal and part time deputy and as soon as they saw the men coming they set two cups of coffee at the table they had chosen to have lunch at. Sherlene wanted to be with her husband while Marilyn was nervous about being with the man she dreamed of. "Do I look alright?" Marilyn asked as she played with her hair. "You look fine!" Sherlene answered playing with her own hair. Sherlene pulled out a chair as she saw the men come through the door, "We're over here!" she said signaling the men to join them at their table. She was smiling as she sat Joe next to Marilyn. Jim knew why his wife was smiling, she enjoyed playing matchmaker! "This should be fun to watch!" he thought with a smile on his face.

Skip and the gunman left the Rocking 'R' ranch late in the morning. They wanted to be at the Crooked Horn by noon, and that would give them all afternoon to find and get rid of his nightmare but little did they know, Joe and the Marshal were just finishing their meal as they walked in and wouldn't be hard to find. Marilyn saw them come through the doors and whispered to Joe, "That's Skip MacCland and his hired gun. I guess we'll know pretty soon who he wants killed!" Joe turned and looked at the men, as far as he knew he had never seen either man before. Larry didn't believe in wasting time, he had things to do and a woman to see. She stood in front of the doors as he stared at Joe. "Stand up!" he ordered, "You killed a friend of mine and now your gonna die!" Now everyone at the table knew who he had been hired to kill because men like Larry had no friends! Joe slid back from the table and looked around the room and then back to Skip, "You're the one who hired him and you're the first one I'm gonna kill!" Joe said confidently. Skip felt a sinking felling in his stomach and his hands were beginning to shake at the words coming from the man's mouth, he wanted to see the man die, he never planned on this being the outcome! Jim sat at the table watching as the men faced each other; "This was not right!" he decided and stood facing Skip, "I've got this one!" he said squaring up to the man. Jim was no gunman and hopefully neither was MacCland! Jim watched as Skips hands flashed towards the pistol, Skip was fast, real fast the pistol was half way out of the holster before Jim's hand touched the butt of his own weapon! Jim knew within a split second he was going to feel the impact of the lead of a forty-four caliber pistol tearing through his body and destroying his life and dreams, at that same time and at that same moment Jim could not think of the reason he had ever become a marshal in the first place but Jim knew one thing for sure, he was about to die! The pistol in Joe's left hand exploded fire and lead flew from the barred striking

Skip in the chest. The half cocked revolver in Skips hand fell to the floor and even as Skip dropped to his knees Joe cocked the pistols again but there was no need Cheatham lay on the floor dead, he had already felt the bite of the bullet from Joe's pistol. Skip leaned back, sitting on the heels of his boots, spurs digging into his flesh, "it's just a dream!" he said as his life's blood ran from his body. Men were dragging the bodies out as Jim sat at the table thinking of how close he had come to dying! If it had not been for the hand speed of the drifter he would have been the one dead on the floor!

Jim unpinned the badge from his shirt and sat at the table staring down at the symbol of law and order, Jim knew he was no gunman and no Marshal! He looked at Sherlene and said, "Those kids will need someone to take care of the ranch until they get back from Mexico. Maybe I'll ride out there and take care of the place for them, they will be needing a foreman, and I think I will apply for the job! Joe sat the table across from him and for the first time since they had met Jim saw real fear in the man and for once in his life Jim knew what someone else was thinking. He may have been a farmer but even he knew Joe was thinking the woman he loved thought of him as nothing more than a gunman, a killer! "I'm no gunman!" Joe said in a voice just above a whisper. Marilyn wrapped her arms around the man she loved trying to comfort him, to ease the torment in his soul, to help bear the sadness of taking a human life. Jim knew no one was going to blame him for what he was about to do, "Your no gunman!" he said as he slid the badge across the table, "You're a Marshal!" Jim took the hand of the woman he loved and together they walked out of the Crooked Horn Restaurant to a new hope and a new life!

It's never easy starting a new life," Jim thought as he rode towards the Malloy ranch. This was not going to be easy either! Better than half a dozen riders still rode for the Malloy brand and some of them would not take kindly to what he was about to do! One of the men sat in a rocking chair on the front porch as he rode up; he was a big man with broad shoulders and powerful hands. Billy's face showed the scars of the bar room brawls that he had been in, he was no gunman; he was a fighter. Bare knuckle or club to club made no difference to him he enjoyed it all. Jim knew the man and knew he was trouble, the barrel of a rifle leaned against the wall behind the rocker. The rifle was for show; Billy liked to hurt people with his hands. "Better to face the man now!" Jim thought than when he has an army behind him. Jim swung down from the roan, "Morning Marshal," Billy said as Jim walked up to the porch. Billy outweighed the ex-Marshal by fifty pounds and he was taking no chances! Jim swung a right with everything he had. Billy saw the blow coming and tried to dodge but the fist landed solid. A look of pain came to his face as the fist struck the jaw and bone cracked and shattered as the side of his head exploded. Billy went down without knowing he had been in a fight. The short barreled forty-four pistol fell from his holster as he bounced off the floor boards and fell to the ground. Jim picked up the pistol and slid it into his own holster; it was a lot better weapon than the colt dragoon he carried. Men like Billy made four times the money real cowboys earned and did nothing in return but cause trouble and bust heads. Jim was sick of the lot of them, "that's for hurting my fist!" he complained as he picked up the rifle, "and this is for making me ride all the way out here to talk you into leaving!" Jim walked through the door of the ranch house with one thought on his mind, "I'm gonna clean this place out!" It was not going to be as hard a job as he thought, there were only two men in the room, one was already passed out and the other was on the way. "What are you doing here?" he demanded. A split second later his head was exploding like the others. Jim may have been smaller and he may have been a farmer but years of hard work had built a strong body. Splitting fence posts with a double headed axes and hauling rocks from the field by hand had made him as hard as the rocks he carried. The power of his arms had crumbled the cowboy as easy as it hauled the stones. The cowboy lost teeth and consciousness as the fist landed. Jim picked up the cowboys pistol and grabbing the man by his boots and began to drag him out the door. "Dang, that boy looks like I hit him!" said a voice from the porch. Jim grabbed the revolver in his holster and swung around, Paul stood on the porch admiring Jim's handy work. "What did you hit him with, a chunk of firewood?" Paul asked as he lifted Billy and draped him over the saddle. "Well are you gonna shoot him or put that thing away?" Joe asked as he sat in the saddle atop the black. "What are you two doing here?" Jim asked surprised that the two men had ridden all the way out to the ranch. "We figured you might have trouble!" Joe said looking at the two men on the floor of the porch, "but I guess they're the ones with the trouble!" Jim rubbed his knuckles, "If you leave the guns out of it I guess I can take care of myself!" Joe looked at the butt of the weapon in Jim's belt, "speaking of weapons, that's a pretty good pistol you're toting, a lot better than the piece of junk you were wearing!" "Well, it was a present; Billy here gave it to me right after he decided to take a nap!" "Do you think he will want it back after he wakes up?" Joe asked. Jim shook his head, "Well if he does we'll talk about it again and I don't think he will want it back a third time!" "I don't think he's gonna be saying much now!" Joe stated dryly, "it looks he's gonna be eating soup for the next three weeks!" Paul came out of the house dragging the drunk, "you must have hit this one with a feather," he said, "I can't find a mark on him any place!" "He was passed out when I got here!" Jim said, "See if you can find their horses will you, I want to get these guys off the ranch." Paul was not the type to take orders but he had known Jim a long time and he was as close to a friend as Paul had. Paul dropped the drunk and started for the barn. It was easy to see the ranch needed a lot of repairs, Jim shook his head and looked at Joe, "This place used to be nice," he said remembering day long gone, "at one time it was the nicest spread in the valley. Malloy and his gang of rats have sure let it go to pot! The barn needs a new roof and some of the boards in the corral need replaced. Someone needs to drag the pond and get the moss and algae out of it!" Joe sat on the back of the black, "Since when does a farmer know so much about ranching?" as he watched Jim's face thinking there is more to this man than a lot of people would guess! As Paul brought two more horses out of the barn Jim informed him that he was not always a farmer, "at one time I was a top hand, took two drives up the Chisholm Trail which was approximately five hundred miles and the second one I was the ram-rod and the boys from the Lazy 'B' ranch rode with me on the second trip!" Joe turned in the saddle to look at the ex-marshal. "Why did you give up cowboying?" he asked. Jim had been asked this question before, it was always the same answer, "Cowboys raise cattle, farmers raise families, it was a choice I had to make and I chose family." "You know times are changing, it is possible to do both!" Joe stated. "That's why I decided to take over here until K.C. and Nicole comes back. It will give me a chance to get the feel of ranching again or at least get my butt toughened up for the twelve hour days in the saddle."

"What do you want me to do with these three?" Paul asked as he pitched the last of the unconscious men over their saddles. "Take them to the edge of the ranch, wake them up and tell them to keep riding and if I catch them on the ranch they will be hung as trespassers or cattle thieves, they can take their choice!" "Kinda harsh ain't it?" Paul asked smiling at the thought of the men dancing from the end of a rope. "That's what they were going to do to that kid K.C., remember that?" Jim said, "And they were the ones who helped put a noose around his neck so it's no better than they deserve!" Jim was talking like the man he had known years ago, the man who had driven a herd of half wild cattle and men from Abilene, Texas to Dodge City, Kansas, this was the man Paul remembered. "You need us to stick around?" Joe asked. Jim shook his head, "Not really!" he said, "The rest of the men are drovers and not the kind of men these guys are. I won't have any problems with them!" "I'll see you later then." Joe said as he turned the black and slapped it with the reins. Paul sat and watched as the black took off, clouds of dirt and dust rose behind the animal. "You'll get used to that!" Jim said as Paul watched in disbelief. "What am I gonna get used to?" Paul asked still not sure what Jim meant. "Riding in the dust!" Jim answered as he headed for the barn; there were a lot of repairs to do. Paul put the spurs to his horse and rode off leading the horses and the unconscious men off the Malloy ranch. "I've got a brand new bar," Paul said talking to the men who lay over their saddle oblivious to the sound of his voice, "She ain't much right now, just a tent and some tables but come a week from now she is gonna be something and if you boys wake up in time you can come on in and I might even buy you your first drink! That is if you can hear me!" he said laughing at the men who wouldn't be in any condition to take him up on his offer anytime soon.

As Paul rode off Jim climbed to the roof of the barn and began tearing off the shingles that had gone bad with age. They were split and cracked and these should have been replaced years ago. Some of them had rotted and his foot went throw in the weaker places leaving large holes where rain and hail would have come through during storms, soaking the horses and grain below. From the roof of the barn Jim saw more of the Malloy riders coming. He was about to find out if these men rode for the brand or for the pay. If they were the kind of men he had just dealt with or real cowboys taking care of the cattle. Jim climbed down off the roof and draw the new pistol several times trying to get used to the feel of the weapon. The barrel was shorter than the colts dragoon, it was at least two pounds lighter than the old blunder bust he had been using and he didn't think he was going to be using this one to drive staples in a fence post or to pound in nails! Jim drew the hammer back, the rolling of the cylinder was smooth and easy, Billy may have been a barroom brawler but if nothing else he knew guns and this was as good as they get. Jim slid the pistol back into the holster and picked up the rifle, checked the loads and then waited for the men to get there; the barrel of the rifle was pointed at the lead rider as they approached. Five men sat staring down the barrel as they brought their horses to a stop. "What are you doing here Marshal?" The leader was a tall man wearing a bright red bandana and a black Stetson. The string of a tobacco pouch hung from his pocket and Jim centered the barrel of the rifle on the dime sized tag on the end of it. "I'm telling you boys to leave." The speaker for the group of men stood up straight in the saddle making the pistol at his side easier to reach, "He ain't the Marshal no more Ray, he said he ain't wearing no badge!" The one called Ray leaned forward, "If you ain't the Marshal you got no authority to run us off!" "No, but I have!" the voice came from behind the ex Marshal. Startled at the sound of the voice behind him, Jim's finger began to tighten on the trigger. The tag on the tobacco pouch was a good target and the man wearing it was about to regret it! Something clicked and Jim recognized the voice, "I thought you had left?" Jim said without bothering to turn around. "When I was riding out I saw these boys riding in and I couldn't very well let you have all the fun so I circled back. After all you snuck up on me once and I just thought I'd return the favor!" Ray stood up in the saddle again, "It don't matter, there's still only two of you and five of us!" "No," Jim said, "When I pull this trigger there is only going to be four of you!" "You're bluffing!" Ray said as he grabbed at the pistol on his side. The roar of the rifle sounded like a small cannon echoing off the walls of the barn and a half inch hole appeared in the center of the tag hanging from the tobacco pouch. Jim knew as the shell passed through the man's body and struck bone the head of the shell would expand, mushrooming and there would be a hole in the man's back large enough to drop a silver dollar through! The power of the bullet picked Ray up and slung him to the ground behind the horse he was riding. Lowering the rifle, the used casing dropped to the ground as a fresh on slid into the chamber and in the flick of a second Joe had filled both hands with cocked revolvers ready to take on the next man to move and Jim's rifle was pointed at the next man in line. "Well?" Jim asked, "Do you want to make it three to two?" Now every man there knew it was no bluff. The four remaining riders sat looking down at their leader, "Not thanks!" one of them said as they turned their horses and headed towards the gate and off the Malloy ranch. "You know you're going to have trouble with them later!" Joe said as he pulled a pouch of tobacco out of his own pocket. Jim took the makings out of his pocket as well and began to build his own cigarette. The paper was yellow with age and Jim poured the tobacco into the folded crease and licked the paper rolling it into a cylinder and then placed it in his mouth and lit the end. Joe was looking at the body as Jim placed the rifle against a fence post and took a hard pull on the stale tobacco, "You know you lied to me?" Joe said. "How's that?" Jim asked. "You told me if you ever shot anyone you'd put ten holes in him to make sure he was dead and Ray here has only got one hole!" "That makes us even, you once told me you were a broken down drifter!" Jim stated.

"If you ain't heading into town right away I'll help you put him in the ice house until I can get the undertaker out here." Joe said. "Either that or we can bury him up on the hill, don't make me much difference." "I guess we can put him in the ice house!" Jim said. "I got a lot of work to do and besides he might have family some place that will want to claim the body!" Both men got a hold of an arm and began to drag the body to the ice house. The cowboys spurs rolled in the dirt kicking up little cloud puffs as he was drag through the yard and into the frigid air of the room, it was midsummer and only small amounts of ice remained. "What are you gonna do now, Joe asked, you ain't got a hand left on the spread?" "I'm here, Jim said, and from what I've seen that's one more hand than they had!" "Maybe it is, Joe answered, but just in case I'[m headed back to town and I'll send some men back to help, if I can find any willing to ride out here!" Jim knew the men that had ridden the cattle trails with him would come to help if he asked but he was not about to ask! "I can handle it, all I need is a few nails and some boards and this place will be up and running in no time!" Joe whistled for the black, it still amazed Jim that the horse was willing to let the man ride him. "One of these days that thing is going to throw you and stomp you!" Jim said as Joe swung up on its back. "Maybe, Joe answered, but one ride is worth the risks!" Joe drew the straps and slapped the side of the black and the animal took off like a jack rabbit, kicking up the clods of dirt Jim had grown accustomed to. Jim had to admit maybe one ride was worth the risks with all of his complaining. He wished he was the one on the back of the black, he would love to be the one leading the pack instead of eating the dust every time the black took off! After Joe left Jim kicked dirt and sand over the blood trail, he did not want the dogs or other animals lapping at the blood. Jim walked into the bunk house and stoked up the stove, some of the coals were still hot so he threw in a couple pieces of wood and placed a pot of water with some beans in it on the front of the stove hoping it wouldn't boil over after he went back on the roof of the barn. The sky was clear and the sun was burning down as Jim climbed to the top and continued tearing the rotted shingles off the neglected building stopping only for a drink of lukewarm water from the canteen at his side. It was a lousy job but someone had to do it and he was the only one left.

After several hours of tearing at the shingles he saw a cloud of dust appear in the horizon, it was from a wagon. He sat on the roof as it drew nearer watching in the distance he could make out the shape of two women he knew; it had to be Sherlene and Marilyn. A second cloud was coming up fast from behind and no one had to tell him it was probably Joe! Jim climbed down from the roof and awaited the arrival of the women. Sherlene looked gorgeous with the afternoon sun dancing off her hair. The new dress she wore showed the curves he loved to admire. Her hazel eyes were shining with the love she held for her husband and Jim knew he was a lucky man to be married to her! Marilyn sat beside her, this was the woman

Joe was in love with and Jim did not blame him, she was a beautiful woman in her own right. The two of them together could take a man's breath away! There was no mistaking they were sisters! Jim walked to the wagon and helped the women down, he held his wife close, it had been a long time since they had been together and Jim missed being in her arms. "Hi honey what brings you ladies out here?" he asked glad for even the few minutes they could be together. Sherlene looked hurt, "You don't think we'd let you do this all alone do you?" She said as she took his arm in hers and headed towards the house. Stopping at the top of the steps Jim and Sherlene stood at the front door watching as Joe brought the black to a halt in front of the house. "Saw a dust cloud from the ridge headed this way; I thought it might mean trouble so I doubled back just to make sure everything was alright." Marilyn stood smiling up at Joe, no cowboy in his right mind rode in a wagon when it was easier to saddle a horse, besides the ride was a lot rougher in the wagon. Marilyn knew he would have seen it was a wagon from a half mile away, she also knew he would have known who was in it! Joe came off the black in one smooth motion, "Can I help you ladies?" he asked as he walked forward to take Marilyn's arm. It was a beautiful afternoon and the women being at the ranch made it even better. Joe took Marilyn's arm and walked with her up the steps. "If Jim doesn't mind I think I'll hang around, maybe pass him up a few shingles if he is still going to be working on the barn roof!" Sherlene knew Joe was not interested in the barn or its roof, "I'm sure Jim is still planning on working on the barn." She said. As she nudged him in the ribs Jim took the hint, "Just as soon as I check on the beans!" he replied. "Sherlene shook her head, "You're not eating beans while we are here!" she said. Sherlene turned to Marilyn, "If you'll run down to the ice house and see if you can find a chicken we can make these boys some mashed potatoes, fried chicken and gravy and if you want we can even whip up a pan of biscuits!" Remembering the body of the man called Ray was still in the ice house, Joe spoke up, "If you don't mind I think I'll see about the chicken while she helps you in the kitchen!" "There's no hurry and I can always throw Jim a few shingles!"

The women started cleaning the kitchen as Joe went in search of a chicken. From the top of the barn Jim heard the cackling of the hens as Joe went into the chicken house and a few minutes later he heard the crack of the axe and the flopping of the bird. It was going to be a while before Jim got any shingles Joe still had to pluck and gut the chicken before he gave it to the women. It was a lot of work for one small bird but it was better than eating anything brought out of the ice house! Jim decided he was going to clean everything out of the ice house after the undertaker left. He was sure between him and Joe they could keep the women out of the room. "It was getting close to dusk before Joe began to pack the shingles up to the barn roof. "I hate chicken!" Joe said as he laid the first bundle down. "Tell that to the women, I'm sure they would not mind going into the ice house for a couple of steaks!" Jim laughed at the thought of the women walking into the dark room with nothing but a lantern and finding the body! He knew they would come out of the room white faced and screaming! "I'll tell them you did it and who do you think they will believe?" Joe dropped the bundles of shingles, "I should have let Skip shoot you!" he said sarcastically as he went down for another load. "Joe, we're going to have to do something about old Ray before the women find him!" Joe put down another bindle, "Tonight we sneak him onto a horse, take him out onto the range and bury him like I wanted to in the first place!" Joe said flatly. "I don't care as long as we get him out of the ice house and away from here, if the women stumble across him we're both cooked!" Joe shook his head it's your funeral if we get caught!" Marilyn came out on the porch and began to ring the dinner bell, "Dinner is ready!" she said as the men climbed down from the barn. It was easy to tell the women had put a lot of work into the meal, a lantern sat in the middle of the table giving the room a cozy look and a romantic feel. Fine linen covered the kitchen table and china and silverware replaced the metal utensils both men were used to lately. Chicken, mashed potatoes and gravy circled the lantern. Sherlene was bringing hot biscuits out of the oven as they entered. The smell of the food filled the room, "Great, I'm starving!" Jim said as he reached for a piece of fried chicken. Marilyn slapped at his hand, "This is not a beer joint or a restaurant, you'll sit down and say grace before we eat!" Jim was forced to oblige, the women had done a lot of work and were proud of the meal they had prepared. "I take it you men are sleeping in the bunk house tonight?" Sherlene said as she filled the plates. Jim knew this last remark was meant for him and it looked like it was going to be another night of sleeping alone. "Yes I guess we are!" Jim answered staring into the plate set before him. At least having Joe spend the night would make it easier to sneak off with the body! Joe tore into the food as Jim pouted over his meal picking at it like a man lost thought. Joe spread a large chunk of butter on one of the hot biscuits. "It isn't that bad, after all you got me for company!" Joe said with a smirk. "Yes and I'm sure there is an old coon dog around here some place too but I ain't interested in sleeping with it either!" Jim growled. Joe laughed out loud at the thought of Jim in all his misery. Sherlene and Marilyn began to blush, "alright you men, out of here, we've got to clean this place up!" Sherlene began to pick up the dishes as Marilyn ushered the men out of the room. Jim took the makings out of his pocket as Marilyn shoved the men out of the house. "You two can stay out here and out of the way until we are done with the dishes, she said, and if you want later we'll put on a pot of coffee!" Joe reached for his own pouch of tobacco as he was leaned against the hitching rail and poured a fine string of tobacco into the crease of the paper, rolled it and lit the end. "Do you think they will come back tonight?" Joe asked as he flicked his cigarette and looked out into the darkness of the night. "If you're talking about the Malloy hands we ran off, I don't think so! The only reason they hung around was because of the free booze they were stealing out of the liquor cabinet, that and the fact they had no place else to go. With old man Malloy dead and the girl gone they weren't making a pay check and what little they had in the bunk house ain't worth fighting or dying for! My guess is they will steal a few head of cattle and head for the border!" "Kinda like the kids did!" Joe said. "Yes, kind of like the kids, the only difference is, I figured Nicole had a right to protect her own property and these guys don't have a right to steal from anybody!" "Well, what are you going to do about it?" Joe asked. "Don't know if I can do anything, there is only one of me with thousands of head of cattle spread out over miles of open range. The Rocking 'R' and the lazy 'B' ranch will both have cattle mixed in with the herd and even with a full crew it would take a week maybe two just to sort out the different brands and separate them from this herd. Then it will take another week to move them closer to the main house so I can keep an eye on them and then I can't watch them night and day!" Joe shrugged, "I could always take a few days off, Rog and Schon can take care of things around town until I get back." "The two of us with the black might be able to bring the herd in closer to the house but we still would not be able to keep a close eye them! Joe agreed. "Well, maybe we could get some help from around town?" Joe said as the women came out of the house carrying coffee for the men. "Keep an eye on what?" They asked at the same time. "The cattle, Joe answered, Jim is worried about losing them!" "Why can't we help, Marilyn could take some time off from the restaurant and we are both good riders?" Sherlene asked thrilled with the idea of helping to round up cattle. Sherlene loved adventure and this sounded like a good one. Marilyn's eyes lit up at the prospect of being around Joe, "Sure we can help, and Terry and Eloise can take care of the restaurant till we get back, without Paul and the drunks being there it will be easy for them to take care of it! Besides, I've been looking for an excuse to take a vacation and this sounds great!" Sherlene and Marilyn went back into the house, making plans on how they could help with the roundup. The rattle of a wagon and the clop, clop of the hooves of the horses could be heard in the distance as the men sat on the porch and drank the coffee. Soon it was apparent the wagon was headed for the Malloy ranch and as it drew nearer Joe reached for the unlit lamp hanging from a nail driven in the beams of the porch and in a few steps Joe was swallowed in the shadows. As the wagon neared, Joe lit the lamp, he was standing behind the trunk of a large oak tree and as the wagon got closer he put the lantern on the ground. This would make him impossible to see from almost anywhere. When the wagon pulled up in front of the house Jim stepped to the corner of the house, the rifle was in his hands as he watched from the shadows. "Hel-low in the house!" came a familiar voice it belonged to one of the young cowboys that loved to terrorize Marilyn. "Bobby, what are you doing out here in the middle of the night?" Jim asked relieved hardly believing that the man would ride this far just for the fun of pestering Marilyn, even if he knew she was here! "Brought you something!" he said. "Who is that in the wagon with you?" Jim asked. Bobby looked kind of sheepish. "This is Michelle, my wife!" Marilyn ran from the house, "When did you get married?" she demanded. Under her sharp eye Bobby wilted, which was really quite funny. "Well, we're not married yet, but we're going to be as soon as we can find a Justice of the Peace!" "You get married without me being there and I'll skin your hide!" she threatened as she stormed back into the house. "And you're not getting married by no Justice of the Peace! You're getting married in a church with a preacher!" Even the thought of one of the cowboys getting married without her being there was enough to infuriate the woman! "I've done everything but change their diapers for them over the years and if they get married without me I'll tan their hides there in the church, right in front of the preacher and the whole congregation!" She told Sherlene as she stormed around the room. Bobby got down from the wagon and then helped his future bride from the wagon. "Maybe you best go inside." Bobby instructed as he removed the tarp from the back of the wagon. "Here is your present boys!" Bobby beamed with pride as he revealed Rick still alive lying in the bottom of the wagon bed. "What am I supposed to do with him?" Jim asked. "I ain't no doctor!" "Well, he rode for the Malloy brand and Malloy is the one who sent him on the ambush that got him cutup. The way I see it the Malloy ranch is responsible for him, besides he's got no kin folk that I know of and as far as I know this is the only place he's got left!" Jim knew Bobby was right, Rick had no kin folks and in a lot of ways he was the same as Joe had been, a homeless drifter riding where ever the jobs took him. Jim grabbed Rick by the heels of the boots and began to pull him from the wagon, "Easy, Bobby said, he still ain't in that gooda shape!" Joe jumped in the wagon and picked Rick up by the shoulders and together they carried Rick from the wagon. "Where are we going to put him?" Joe asked. "He ain't dead yet so we might as well put him in the bunkhouse." Bobby held the door open as the men carried Rick inside. "I got some medicine for him in the wagon." Bobby said as they laid Rick on one of the bunks; Rick had not so much as flinched as he was being carried! "What are you giving him?" Joe asked surprised that the man was still unconscious after the rough handling of the move. "A mix of whisky and opium, called Laudanum." Bobby climbed into the wagon and did as he was instructed "Why would anybody load ice in the middle of the night?" Bobby asked as the men went through the door. Joe turned around, "Shut up, we don't want the women to know what we are doing!" Bobby set on the wagon seat and watched as Joe and Jim loaded the body of the dead man into the wagon. "Crap, if Michelle sees that she is gonna jump out of the wagon and walk home!" Bobby complained. Both men spoke up at the same time, "Then keep him covered!" Jim jumped up on the back of the wagon and began to pull the tarp over the body, "Hold on a minute!" Joe said as he climbed into the back. "If you ain't superstitious you'll need this!" Joe said as he undid the gun belt from around the dead man. Jim looked down at his own gun belt; the fast draw holster with the bullet loops sown into the belt was a lot better than the rig he wore. It was a pain in the butt carrying the shells for the new gun in his pocket and the powder flask, ball and caps to the old gun were a pain to get to plus the old pistol was slow to load, "Thanks!" Jim said taking the new gun; maybe it would bring him more luck than it had its predecessor! Joe took the spurs off the dead man's boots because the grinding of the spurs was sure to give away the fact that someone was in the back of the wagon and if they wanted to sneak Ray out it had to be done! Jim turned back to Bobby, "After you drop Michelle off take him to the undertakers, he will know what to do with him and after that see if you can get a couple of men to come out here and give us a hand, we need to move the cattle closer to the ranch house!" "Will do!" Bobby said as he pulled the wagon away from the ice house, it would not pay for the women to see where he was parked and get suspicious and the last thing in the world Bobby wanted was for Michelle to look into the back of the wagon! The women came out of the house as Bobby pulled up. "It's getting late," Sherlene said, "Why don't you spend the night that way you can always leave in the morning?" Bobby felt stuck and didn't know what to say, "That would be fine, Jim said but he has tot to get back to town, he's going to send us some men to help with the round up and we'll need them in the morning and besides I don't want him rushing cause I knowed a fellow one time rushing around in the dark that lost half his load!" Michelle climbed into the wagon and set next to Bobby, "I don't mind riding around on the dark with Bobby!" she said snuggling up next to the man besides her. "Besides the only load we have is that dumb tarp and I don't care if we lose it or not!" Jim took Sherlene around the waist and pulled her close, both couples stood and watched as Bobby pulled the wagon out of the yard, "By mom!" Bobby cried as they rode out into the darkness hopping to get one more rise out of Marilyn before they vanished from sight.

Michelle snuggled up closer to Bobby, she had heard the remark Bobby had made to Marilyn about them being married and if she had her way it was going to be true, he was going to pop the question for real and she was going to be engaged before the night was over! This was a beautiful Texas night, the stars were shining under a full moon and she was riding with the man she loved and if there was a more romantic setting she had never seen it! Bobby held the reins in his left hand while his right arm was around Michelle pulling her closer. He liked the feel of her body next to his and the way she smiled and even the color of her eyes! Maybe tonight he would ask her to marry him, after all what could be more romantic than a moon light buggy ride?

"I hope they make it!" Joe said as he tuned to walk away. "What is that supposed to mean?" Marilyn asked. "Nothing, Joe answered, but it's dark out there and anything could happen!" "Yes, they could even lose the tarp!" Jim said laughing at the thought of Michelle finding the body and freaking out in the dark! Boy, Bobby was going to have his hands full if that happened, he thought to himself.

All three of the men riding behind Paul had managed to wake up before they reached town and they didn't have to be told they were tied to their saddles. The bindings on their feet and wrists told them all they needed to know. The bouncing of the horse had made the drunk sick and he was throwing up on the saddle. Vomit and booze was running down the side of the horse, "let me up!" he cried choking in his own waste! Paul stopped the horses and walked back to the men where he began to cut them loose one at a time. The bindings had been tight and the men had lost circulation in their arms and feet. Paul had to catch them as they unloaded and then place them on the ground until they were strong enough to stand on their own. "What happened? One of them demanded to know. "You got run off the Malloy ranch!" Paul informed them. "Where's my gun?" the one who had been drunk was asking. "It's back at the ranch and if I was you I would forget it!" Paul was beginning to lose his patients. "What do you mean?" again it was the drunk with the belligerent attitude. "Look, three things are gonna happen if you ride back! One, Jim said he would hang any one of you caught back on the Malloy ranch! Now I don't think he is going to do that but what I do think is he is gonna bust you upside the head as hard as he can then he is gonna pound on you for a while and in that case you gonna look worse than your buddy here! Two, that gun slinging pal of his is gonna give you back your gun then make you use it! One way or another you still ain't gonna have that gun and you might wind up dead!" The drunk stood up and tried to clear his head, "I'm going back for my gun!" he stated. Paul shook his head, "it sure ain't a good day for the Malloy riders is it?" The drunk turned around to look at Paul as he drew back his fist and let it fly. The drunks head looked as if it was attached to his shoulders with a rubber band as the massive fist landed, driving it backwards, almost to the point of breaking! "Three, is for the doctor as Paul loaded the man over his saddle and tied the bindings, "Well do you two want to ride sitting up or laid over?" Neither man wanted to move but then again neither wanted to ride draped over their horse either! "We're coming!" they grumbled as they climbed to their feet and mounted the horses. Paul stroked the horse carrying the unconscious man, "Sorry about that!" he said felling sorry for the animal. "When we get back to town I'll make sure you get cleaned up!" the unconscious man woke up just before they entered the town, he began to complain but this time it fell on deaf ears and he was no longer drunk and his head felt as if it had been hit with the blunt end of a pole axe. "You're trying to kill me!" he complained. "If you don't like the treatment keep your mouth shut!" Paul said as he pulled up to the tent that served as a bar. "If you boys want to come in I'll buy you a drink!" Two of them shook their head slowly trying not to increase the pain. Paul cut the third man lose with the knife at his side, "you coming in?" he asked as the man put his boot in the stirrups and pulled at the reins, "Not from you!" he said as he started to pull away. Paul reached up and grabbed the man by the arm and pulled and this time he was not gentle, the man landed flat on his back in the street, "I told that horse I'd see to it that it would get cleaned up when we reached town and that is just what I plan to do, so you either walk him over to the trough and give him a bath or I'll do it for you!" The side of the man's head was red and bruised and there was a large knot that took up most of his face. He was trying to catch his breath from the fall but he was still belligerent, "And if I don't give him a bath then I'll bust you harder than Jim ever would have!" Paul threatened. As the men rode off Paul walked into the bar and saw Nita behind the make shift bar selling drinks, "What are you doing here?" he asked as she handed him a shot glass filled with the good liquor from below the bar. Nita put on her best smile, "It's the least I could do for my new partner!" Nita filled her own glass and tapped it against his and took a sip. Paul was about to explode, "What do you mean, new partner?" "Well, Nita said, I heard you've been trying to hire some of my girls and if that is the case I figure we're going to be partners, either that or I'm gonna start selling booze at my place!" Nita smiled again, "It shouldn't take long for me to put you out of business!" Paul knew she spoke the truth and he didn't have the funds to go against the woman, his dreams of being a private owner and the Lord of his own domain was over. This woman had the money to bury him! At the very least she could put him out of business for good.

Bobby and Michelle took the buggy and wagon road back into town, it was a longer ride but Michelle didn't mind she just snuggled up closer to her future husband. Bobby didn't mind because it was smoother and there was less chance of bouncing around their cargo, even if it was longer. The town was deserted as they drove up, even Paul's make shift bar was closed. Several dogs began following the wagon and howling at the top of their lungs. Michelle tried to shoo them away but they became more aggressive and some even tried to jump into the back of the wagon. "What is wrong with these crazy dogs!" she screamed as they ran alongside. Bobby took out his pistol and fired a round into the ground in front of the dogs. The dogs took off running at the sound of the revolver and the smack of the bullet landing beside their paws. Michelle watched as the dogs ran, some forward and other back. The street lamps lit the back of the wagon, the tarp had moved during the night and the toe of one boot showed from beneath the tarp. "I thought we dropped Rick off?" she said as she pulled back the tarp to check on the man. Ray lay face up, his dead eyes stared up into the heavens and it only took a second for Michelle to realize this was not Rick and a dead man lay in the back of the wagon. Michelle turned on him with flailing fists, swinging at his face and arms, "How could you?" she screamed as she swung at the man. "Stop it!" Bobby yelled. Between the dogs, the gun fire and Michelle's screams the horses were acting up and he was having a hard time controlling them. As Bobby yelled they bolted, tearing through town at break neck speeds, "You're going to get us killed!" he cried as he fought for control of the runaway team. Bobby had fought runaway teams before but never in the middle of the night and never with a hysterical woman trying to claw his eyes out! He was pleading with her to stop and he knew he couldn't push her away because she might fall out of the wagon and get run over. He was doing his best to bring the team under control and his soon to be bride at the same time! He spoke again, this time in a lower voice, "Stop it honey before you kill us both!" this time Michelle listened and stopped the beating, she even pulled herself against Bobby and held on as he fought the frightened horses, "Stop them!" she begged as the wagon rocked from side to side. He set the break with his foot as he pulled with all his strength against the reins. Bobby felt the horses turn to the right so he jerked the reins to the left. The wagon was up on two wheels as the horses tuned then rocked and came up on the opposite two wheels, "Hang on!" Bobby cried as the wagon launched forward and they were being bounced around on the wagon seat as it hit the ruts in the road. "We're gonna crash!" Michelle cried as Bobby fought the team. Lights were coming on as they charged through town. Ray bounced out of the wagon and into the street. The dogs were no longer interested in Ray they were doing their best to get out of the way of the runaway wagon. The lead horse stumbled and fell dragging the animal next to him down into the dirt. They skidded in the dirt as the wagon tongue slid beside them. The wagon came to a stop with chains and braces locked tight but still on its wheels! Bobby hopped down and ran to the horses; they were trying to stand even as he approached. Michelle was climbing down from the wagon, "Quick! Bobby said, go get the doc!" "You mean the vet?" Michelle asked. "They're the same thing!" Bobby said, "Just go get one of them!" Michelle ran towards the stables! The horses were standing as Paul came running up, "What can I do to help?" he asked as Bobby ran his hands over the animals, checking for broken bones. "Will you go get the undertaker?" Bobby asked. "Why, Paul wanted to know, the horses weren't dead! Did you run somebody over?" "No, Bobby answered, he was shot!" "Who did you kill?" Paul demanded trying to understand how he could shoot someone while fighting a terrified pair of horses. "I didn't kill anyone, Jim did!" "Jim could not have killed anyone, Paul answered, he is out at the Malloy ranch!" "I know he is out at the ranch, that's where he killed Ray!" "Who is Ray?" Paul wanted to know. Ray is the guy Jim killed!" Bobby replied. "Well then why do you need an undertaker?" Paul persisted. "Because Ray is laying out in the street!" Bobby said. "If Jim killed him at the ranch how come he's lying in the street?" Paul was curious. "Look, Bobby said, Jim shot him at the ranch and I brought him to town in the wagon and he got pitched out when the horses bolted and he is laying out there now! So could you go get the undertaker and pick him up before someone else steps on him?" No one ever said Paul was the sharpest person on the planet, Bobby thought but he might as well have been talking to a tree stump but in the end he finally understood, "Sure, he said, why didn't you say so in the first place!" Paul took off running as Bobby continued to check on the horses. Doc was young but well trained; he took over Bobby's place and began to check the horses. "They will be alright." He said after checking the bumps and bruises. "What about Ray?" Bobby asked. "Paul dragged him off the street; he will be alright until I get there." "What are you going to do with him?" Bobby asked. "Put him in the ice house for tonight and tomorrow we'll bury him." The doctor answered. "Great! Bobby said, that's where I picked him up from!" "Now, if you will excuse me, I'm headed to bed! In the excitement Bobby had forgotten how late it was, "Sorry about waking you up, he said, it's just that I was afraid one of the horses might have broken a leg or something!" "Don't worry about it, he answered, a couple of cowboys from the Malloy ranch woke me up earlier, one of the men looked like he had been kicked in the face by a bull and I had just finished wiring his jaw shut when you decided to charge through town!" "Thanks again, doc." Bobby said as the man left heading on his way home for a much needed rest.

"What are you gonna do now?" Michelle asked not sure if there was anything they could do. "Well, the first thing to do is unhitch the horses and put them in the stable, their gonna need feed and water after the night they have had and after that I'm headed out to the Lazy 'B' ranch to get Roy and Mike up. I figure their gonna want to help with the round up on the Malloy ranch. You might as well go home and get some rest because I'll be with them for the next few days trying to get the herd together. Paul stepped out from the group of men that had gathered around the wagon, "I'll buy you two a drink before you leave, it will help settle the shakes!" "I've got to take care of the horses first, you two go have a drink and I will join you as soon as I can." Bobby said. Schon came up about that time and took the horses by the reins, "Don't worry about them, I'll take care of the horses, you two go have that drink." Schon said as he started walking the horses to the stables and after wiping them down and putting salve on the cuts, Schon gave them some grain and water. It was turning out to be a long night for the deputy. He would be glad when things quieted down, all he wanted to do was go back to the office, kick his feet up and sleep for the rest of the night!

Bobby tossed the second shot of the strong tequila down as Paul poured himself a third, "That's all I can have, Bobby said, I've got a long ways to go! If I drink a third I might not be going anywhere!" Michelle sipped at her second drink but hers was no shot glass, she drank from a large beer glass. Bobby took her hand, "Come on honey, it's time to go." He said as Michelle signaled for a third. Michelle turned like a caged panther, her honey sweet eyes blazed with anger Bobby had never seen before, "We were engaged! She cried as she began swinging at the man in a half drunken rage. Bobby wrapped his arms around her, this time it was not an embracement of love, it was an act of survival! She was trying to tear his eyes out with her claws and Bobby was forced to hang on for dear life! "How fast life changes, he thought, it was less than an hour ago he had stopped the wagon on top of the hill overlooking the town where he had gotten down on one knee and proposed. It was the perfect setting, Michelle looked so innocent at the time, and the smile on her face had lit up the sky as she accepted his proposal. He had held her in his arms marveling at how lucky he was now he was terrified that if he let go she was going to scratch out his eyes! Paul watched the fight with excitement, he loved a good fight and this was stacking up to be a good one! "Have another drink," Paul said pouring a third as Bobby held Michelle in his arms. Paul knew the more she drank the madder she would become and he looked forward to the fight. Bobby held Michelle in his arms until she calmed down then took a drink from the glass, this time his was not shot glass but a beer mug. Michelle picked up her own drink and downed what was left and swung the mug at Bobby's head. Paul was right, the more she drank the madder she got. She could not believe Bobby had held her in his arms and told her how much he loved her, then got down on his knee and proposed to her all the while knowing there was a corpse in the back of the wagon! She was crying hysterically, "The wedding is off!" she screamed. This time Bobby could not believe what he was hearing, Michelle ran from the bar as Bobby stood in a trance, how could she do this to him? Didn't she know how important she was to him? Paul poured another shot of tequila and sat and watched as Bobby stood in disbelief, "She will come back, he said, after she cools down!" Bobby was not so sure, "How do you know? Bobby asked. "I know women, Paul said, and I know she loves you, she will be back!" "Great, now I'm taking advice about love from a lonely old bar tender that looks like a large blonde haired gorilla!" Bobby had never felt so desperate or alone in his life, "Could my life get any worse?" he thought as he reached for the glass in front of him. He was ready to start crying into the empty glass as Schon walked in, "Alright close up!" he said. Bobby tried to stand, "It's alright, I'm leaving anyway!" he said as Paul started to object. Schon watched as Bobby staggered through the door, "What's wrong with him?" Schon asked seeing the look of pain on Bobby's face. "Girl troubles!" Paul said and that was all Schon needed to know, "maybe I better keep an eye on him." Schon said as he started out the door. Young men with girl problems could do desperate things! Schon watched as Bobby made his way to the stables and it was apparent he was not used to the strong bite of the tequila.

    Apple shied away as Bobby walked into the stall, it seemed the horse was not used to the smell of the tequila either! Bobby stroked the animal's neck trying to calm her down. Apple was a small black and white Paint with one white stocking. She was too small to hold a thousand pound bull tied to her saddle with a rope but she was a good cutting horse, quick and agile. During the fall Bobby collected wild apples that grow on the Lazy 'B' ranch for the horse, they were her favorite food and she would follow the man around all day for one bite or one small apple, this was the reason Bobby called her Apple. Schon watched as Bobby picked up the saddle and lost his balance. Stumbling backwards Bobby slammed against the boards of the stall, slid down and wound up sitting on his butt with the saddle in his lap! "How about I help you to the hotel?" Schon offered as he picked the saddle up off the man. Bobby had never been this drunk in his life; the barn was spinning from the bite of the tequila as Schon helped him to his feet. "Can't, Bobby said, I've going to tell Mike and Rou that we got to help Jim and the gunfighter round up cattle tomorrow!" Schon shook his head, "even if I saddled you're horse for you, I don't think you could make it out the barn door, much less to the ranch! It's either the hotel or the jail, your choice!" unlike his partners Bobby was not much of a drinker and until tonight he had thought of himself as a lover but after the night he just had he was not so sure of that either. "I've never been in jail." He said as Schon led him out the stable doors. "You're not going to be locked up, Schon explained; all I want to do is get you some place where you'll be safe. I don't want you hurting yourself until after you're sobered up!" Bobby stumbled along as Schon led him to the jail, "You ain't gonna lock it?" Bobby asked as Schon laid him on the bunk in the cell. Bobby lay on his side and pulled his knees up to his chest, "I'm gonna be sick!" he said as the room began once again to spin. This was the worse ride he had ever been on! "I ought to bust Paul upside the head for giving you that much tequila!" Schon said as he handed Bobby a hot cup of the strong black coffee. "Sit up and have a real drink, it might make you feel better!" Schon knew it was going to take a while for the coffee to do any good but might as well get a good start!

Nita was having her own problems, as Michelle lay in her arms sobbing, "Bobby asked me to marry him and I said yes!" Nita did not understand, "Wasn't that what you wanted?" Nita was still confused, "if you did not want to marry the cowboy why did you say yes?" "I do want to marry him, Michelle answered, but I broke off the engagement!" "Why would you break off the engagement if you wanted to marry him?" This was making no sense to the woman. "He was hiding a dead man in the wagon behind me all the while he was telling me how much he loved me. He did not even tell me and if it weren't for the dogs barking I might have never known. Then he took a shot at the dogs and made the horses bolt! I was on a runaway wagon that almost killed me all because of him and his stupid dead body! How could I ever trust a man like that?" Nita stroked her hair as she sobbed in her arms, she knew they were a far cry from Bobby's arms and Michelle needed to be in his arms but this was the best she could do. Nita knew there was going to be no sleeping tonight and it was going to be a long lonely night for both of them.

Joe awoke with the feeling that he had never felt so alive, every fiber of his body felt the love he felt for the woman waiting for him in the house and he almost sang as he got out of the bed. It was a gorgeous day and it was about to get better, he was going to see the woman he dreamed of. The smell of mesquite logs being burned in the wood stove lingered in the air and found its way into the bunk house, he could even smell bacon being fried in an iron skillet. He picked up the small water bowl and filled it with water and soaped up the rag that served as a wash cloth and hanging the mirror on the handle of the stove damper Joe began to shave using the four inch piece of honed steel known as a straight razor. Rick was sleeping in the bed next to the wood burning stove; Joe put down the razor, dried the soap off his face with the rag and walked over to his bed. The man didn't look good so Joe pulled back the bandages covering the knife wound. It had been bad; a ten to twelve inch gash ran just below Rick's neck. The blade had bitten deep cutting along the ribs to the bone and across the shoulder. It was a clean cut and the kids had done a good job stitching it up but Rick had lost a lot of blood. Joe could see no sign of infection so he covered the wound with the bandages, maybe later he would wash it and change the bandages and put clean ones on but for now the think Rick needed most was rest, that and all the liquids the women could get him to drink. Rick began to groan from the pressure of Joe's hand replacing the bandage and as Joe started to step back Rick's eyes opened. The look of both fear and shame crossed his face, "Who are you?" he asked as his eyes focused on Joe, this was a man he didn't know. "I'm not the one who did this!" Joe said pointing at the gash in his shoulder. "I know." Rick said as his mind went back to the night of the knifing. Even in his weakened state he remembered the look on Frank's face as he had attacked him. "That was Frank!" he said. "I killed a man once, he said, it was years ago in Dallas. I was young then and it was a fair fight but I could never shake the shame of taking another life and I swore it would never happen again but I guess I was wrong, I was supposed to help kill some kids but I could never have done it. I guess Frank figured that one out and decided to shut me up and when Frank tried to kill me I killed him instead. I didn't want to but he forced me into it, it was either kill or be killed!" Joe shook his head; there was no sense in letting the man torture himself, "Frank won't be back, the men he rode with took care of that!" "What about them, Rick asked, they will be looking for revenge!" "No they won't, we buried them south of the border, and they won't be looking for anybody, ever! Joe could see that Rick was tired, "Get some sleep," he said as he gently pushed the man over on his side. "I'll check on you later," he promised as he headed out the door. The sun had risen over the horizon as Joe headed for the barn; it was turning out to be a beautiful morning. Barn swallows dove at his head as he entered the door of the barn trying to drive him away from the nests they had hidden in the rafters. Even the sound of the desert owl could be heard in the distance. The black trotted up to the barn as he saw Joe approach, he knew it was feeding time and he looked forward to the small scuffle he would have with the man feeding him. Over the oats, the horse loved to shove at him with his head and the feel of the man's hands as he scratched him behind the ear. This man was not his master, he was his friend.

That morning was one of the mornings Joe was right, some animals do wake up in a better mood than some people and this was one of those mornings. Jim woke up in a lousy mood; he pulled his shirt gently over the red blisters covering his back. He could not believe that he had burned that fast or that bad. After Joe and Paul left he had removed his shirt exposing the white flesh of his skin to the merciless southwest Texas sun and as he tore the shingles from the barn. It had only been for a few hours at best and in return it had turned his skin into a bright crimson color. Small blisters covered his back and shoulders. This was not going to be one of his better days and even the smell of the mesquite coming from the kitchen stove or bacon frying in the pan did nothing to help his disposition. All he wanted was a cup of coffee and maybe some ice to lay across his back. Glancing at the bunks he could see that Joe had already gone his boots, hat and pistols were missing. He was not surprised; it had been a restless night because of the burns and the fact that he had heard Joe talking to Rick. Jim ran the razor up and down the leather strap putting a fine edge on the piece of steal before he began to shave. The last thing he wanted was a face full of cuts to go along with the blister! Rick lay in the bed watching as Jim finished shaving, taking his right hand he felt along his own face and realized it had been more than a few days since it had felt the touch of a razor. "Do you think I could borrow that," he asked. Jim watched as the shaking hand went back to the man's side, he was in no mood to watch the man cut his own throat and he was in no mood to shave the man himself! "Maybe tomorrow," Jim said as he laid the razor next to the bowl that served as a wash basin. He was tired, he was hungry and he wanted to see his wife! He knew Joe was already going to be in the kitchen drinking coffee and eating breakfast and he might even be laughing and going on with the women. Maybe Jim was a little jealous, after all he was the one who was married so why was he sleeping in the bunk house with the rest of the men when he could be spending the nights in the loving arms of his wife! It was turning out to be a miserable morning; with the blisters on his back he doubted if the day was going to be any better than the night. Joe was exiting the barn as Jim walked out of the bunk house. Joe looked in a good mood for a person that was about to spend his day chasing wild cattle out of a Texas draw or dodging the horns of the always dangerous cattle known as the long horn but of course Joe was going to be riding in the saddle on the back of the black! For the next few days his life was not going to be easy but it was going to be an adventure! Joe was in a good mood and smiling as he slapped Jim on the back, "Are you ready for this?" he asked as he headed through the door. Jim was not ready for anything but hated to show a weakness in front of the gunman and Marshal he considered a friend. "As ready as I'll ever be!" he stated through clenched teeth and winching from the pain of the slap to his back.

Sherlene wore a pair of Levi's, boots and a bandana was tied around her neck and the broad brim of the Stetson hung over the arm of a chair. Even in the men's attire she was beautiful, the curves beneath let everyone know this was no man! This alone brought a smile to Jim's face; maybe today was not going to be so bad after all!

Joe only had eyes for the woman standing beside her and like Sherlene; Marilyn was dressed in the same working attire. The yellow bandana tied around her neck set a golden tint to her light brown hair. It was with difficulty that Joe made his way to the table, every fiber of his being wanted to take the woman in his arms and tell her how much he loved her! Joe sat at the table watching the women work around the kitchen and the smell of bacon, eggs and pancakes filled the room. The coffee was black and strong just the way he liked it. Sherlene and Marilyn sat sipping coffee as the men attacked the hot breakfast with a ravenous appetite. Marilyn set aside her cup, "how is Rick," she asked. Joe was the one she was looking at and for a just a second he felt a tinge of jealousy, "How would I know!" he answered and for a split second he regretted the answer. This was not what he had meant to say, this made him look cold and hard and that was not the impression he wanted to give to the woman sitting next to him! Marilyn knew there was a softer side to the man but it had been buried deep a long time ago. "I'll go check on him," she answered. Joe felt the flair of anger and jealousy at the thought of her being in the room with the injured man. "I'll check on him later!" he answered. "Don't bother!" Marilyn said sarcastically, "I'll check on him now!" Joe could not help the jealousy raging in his heart, why was he acting so stupid? "Why bother, he asked, the guy ain't nothing but a bush whacker and cattle thief and they should have hung him from the first limb they came across!" Joe could not believe he was saying this. Why was he trying to pick a fight with the woman he loved and planned on marrying, yet he was deliberately trying to antagonize her! "He is no bushwhacker and no murder, Marilyn snapped at him, I don't believe he ever would have killed anyone, he is just a man who grew too old and was forced to do whatever he was told!" Marilyn stomped out of the room fuming at the man she was in love with, "How could he be so cold?" she wondered as she headed for the bunk house.

Rick lay on the bed watching as Marilyn came through the door with a tray in her hands and it was easy to tell she was upset. "What's the matter?" he asked as she set the tray down and began to remove the bandages, "Nothing!" she said as she pulled at the last of them, she was on the verge of crying and Rick winched in pain as the last one came off. "Maybe I had better wait for the other fellow," Rick said as Marilyn poked and prodded at the wound. "What makes you think they are any better at this than I am?" she said still fuming at the callus remark Joe had made. Rick let loose with a cry of pain, he was better this morning!" "Who was better this morning?" she asked astonished. "Don't know his name, never met him before but he was the fellow with the cross-draw holster." "If he checked on you why did he tell me he did not what condition you were in today?" "Don't know, Rick confided, love does make a man say strange things sometimes!" Marilyn began to calm down, maybe he was not as cold and callus as he tried to appear! Marilyn went back to cleaning the wound but this time she was a lot more gentle. Rick thought about asking for a shave but that might have been pushing his luck and if Joe was the jealous type he did not want to get tangled up in that mess!

Sherlene had finished washing the dishes as Marilyn came into the house, "Are you ready for this?" she asked as she put down the dish rag and placed the dark brown Stetson on her head. Marilyn was not only ready she looked forward to the adventure, "You bet!" she said as she reached for her own hat. Hers was black with a silver band, she knew it was an expensive hat and not really the kind a person wore on a trail drive or a round up, she had ordered it from a magazine. She remembered waiting for it with anticipation, it took six weeks for the hat to arrive and this was the first time she would be able to wear it without looking out of place. Marilyn placed the hat on her head with just a little tilt, "Wait until Joe sees this," she thought as she admired herself in the mirror. "Come on we ain't got all day to admire ourselves!" Sherlene said thinking sure Marilyn looked good but so did she! Both women started out the door at the sound of a wagon coming to a stop in front of the house. This was not the job they had volunteered for! Jim pulled a large chuck wagon up to the front porch, "Here you go ladies," he said as he stepped down from the wooden plank that served as a seat. The canvas tarp over the wagon looked like the sail of a ship at sea, blown tight from a strong wind. One thing for sure neither one of the women wanted to be the captain of this ship. Jim could not help seeing the expression of disgust on their faces, "Relax ladies Joe's saddling your horses now, and I'm the one riding the blister end of this thing. I was hoping you would stock it for me though? I ain't the best cook on the planet and I'd probably forget half the things we would need." "There are just four of us, Sherlene said, how much do you think we will need?" "There are four of us now, Jim said, but there will be later!" "How many more?" Sherlene asked. "Well if my guess is right Roy and Mike are going to show up plus Paul and Bobby, that makes eight of us altogether and there is a chance of a few others, granted not much of a chance but a chance. That means you will have to pack enough food for at least eight people for a week!" "We don't mind packing it as long as we don't have to ride in it and we are not going to do all of the cooking either!" If Jim had ever entertained thoughts of them volunteering to drive the wagon those thoughts were now gone! Sherlene started a list, "We'll need flour, bacon, beans, eggs, sugar and coffee." There was a lot of food to be gathered but the women knew their jobs and it was a lot better than Jim would have done and if it was left up to him everyone would be eating beans for the next week. Joe brought three horses out of the barn as the women were loading the wagon. One of them was a light chestnut color with two white stockings, one was a beautiful black and white paint and the third was Jim's horse following behind the others. "I didn't think the women were gonna volunteer to ride on the wagon so I didn't saddle your horse." Joe informed him. "Thanks, Jim said, now I have to walk back to the barn for my saddle!" Joe didn't mind the little remark, "That will teach you to put me in jail!" Joe joked as Jim started back to the barn. The women had finished loading the wagon as Jim came back with his saddle and bridle and after placing those in the wagon Sherlene informed him that they would need some meat for the round up. Neither man wanted to eat anything from the ice house. "We'll kill it on the way!" Joe said as Marilyn started towards the ice house door. "What about Rick, Sherlene asked, we can't just leave him; he will starve to death before we get back, even if he doesn't get an infection." Rick was something Jim had not planned on; Mike or Roy should be here by tomorrow." He said. "What does he do until then, lay there and suffer, Sherlene asked, and what if they don't come, he can't get up[and make his own meals, he will starve to death in that bed, if he doesn't die of thirst first!" "Great, why is everyone asking me these questions, Jim thought, why had I not stayed a farmer? This was not even his war, "What am I supposed to do, he wondered, fine, we'll put him in the wagon for now, at least I'll have some company! Jim growled as he looked at Sherlene. Sherlene smiled sweetly at her husband, there's no way she was going to ride in the wagon! "Can you back that thing?" Joe asked as Jim climbed aboard. "I can back it as soon as you get those horses out of the way, Jim snarled! Jim began to back the wagon up to the door of the bunk house just as soon as Joe moved the other horses out of his way. "You're one lucky man, Jim said, you're about to spend the next week with two beautiful women!" Rick didn't know what he meant but anything was better than lying in the bed for the next week. "What do you mean?" he asked. "You're going on a cattle drive," Jim said. Rick could not believe his ears but his eyes lit up at the prospect, it had been almost five years since he had ridden the range like a real cowboy, even if it was in the bottom of a wagon, at least he could smell the aroma of the open fire and he would be able to watch the night sky as the stars flicker over head and hear the cry of the lonely coyote looking for a mate. This was the life Rick had left behind as he grew older and this was the life he missed! It didn't matter how he got there as long as he could go one more time, he would give anything to be on a real cattle drive with men he respected and in the process earn respect back again for the first time in years. He wanted to die an honest man, a man he could look at in the mirror and not be disgusted. With Jim's help Rick managed to stand and then he began to walk, this was an adventure he did not want to miss out on. Joe pulled Rick into the wagon and laid his head on Jim's saddle, it wasn't the best pillow in the world but Rick didn't mind one bit, he had used them before. There was a pistol belt hung beside Rick's bunk, "this is probably yours, Jim said, the pistol was probably taken when you were delirious and if you will hang on a second I'll see if I can find you a new one." Jim went into the ice house and after stumbling around in the dark for a few minutes he came out carrying out what he went in for, the revolver that had fallen out had fallen out of Ray's holster. Rick looked at the pistol; it was pearl handled with several notches on the handle. He knew the owner of the weapon but before he could ask about it Joe cut in, "Don't worry nobody is going to come looking for it." "That was a relief, the former owner had been a hot head that Rick thought was crazy and if the man was still alive, being in possession of the revolver could have gotten him killed. Rick sat back admiring the weapon as Jim climbed on board. There was no need to crack the whip; the teams of horses behind the harnesses were ready for whatever lay ahead. Jim had to lean back to reach the wheel brake and after jerking back the brake was released. The horses started forward and the journey was about to begin. It may have been an adventure to the others but for Jim it was a journey. There were still small bands of hostile Indians roaming the area plus Texas had more snakes than any place he had ever seen. Rattlesnakes, water moccasins, coral snakes, cottonmouths and copperheads all lived in Texas. He had even heard of a lizard called a gilamonster. It was said to be short and stocky with an orange belly and its bite was deadly as any snake. He had never seen one and was not even sure if it really existed but it was one more thing to keep an eye out for these were just natural enemies. There were still the rustlers and thieves and flat out killers that roamed the deserts and hills looking for a victim. It was a journey filled with all the dangers of a cattle drive.

A large jack rabbit bolted towards the Texas desert as the wagon rolled through the arched gate that led to the main house of the Malloy ranch. From here miles and miles of desert stretched across the landscape. This was wild country, open range and every man and animal there was as free and dangerous as the west Texas wind blowing across the prairie. From his perch on top of the wagon Jim could see dark clouds forming in the north. Lightning flashed across the sky and to the ground below. Soon the ditches and draws would be filled with the raging waters known as a flash flood, anything and anyone caught in the draws would be swept away, killing cattle, horses and riders alike. This was one of the most feared things in

Texas, nature at its worst. The water would fill the ditches long before the storm reached the wagon but when it got there it would come down in sheets soaking anything in its path. Lightning would dance around the wagon like giant balls of light, killing anything it touched. The women might tie their horses to the back of the wagon and climb inside for the comfort and safety of the tarp covered wagon but he had no doubt Joe would drape a parka over his shoulders pull down the wide brim of his hat protecting his eyes as the storm struck and together he and the black would face nature's fury head on. Jim hoped the women had not ridden so far ahead that they could not get back to the wagon before the storm struck and before the draws filled and left them stranded to face the storm alone and without shelter. Jim could feel the temperature drop as the storm approached. He knew the snakes and lizards would be hiding in burrows and under rocks trying to escape the fury of the storm. Even as the first drops fell he saw the women ride over the horizon and he knew Joe would not be far behind. Lightning flashed across the sky as the women reined in next to the wagon, it was their choice, don the ponchos and face the storm or climb into the wagon and wait it out! These were massive clouds moving at high speeds, the storm would be strong and powerful but short in its rage. Joe rode up to the wagon and donned a poncho as the women climbed inside for the protection of the covered wagon. Small pieces of hail began to pound the ground as the storm grew nearer, the canvas of the tarp popped in the wind as it was blown from side to side, even the horses tied to the rear of the wagon tried to escape the storm pulling at their reins as lightning struck the ground in a long flash of fire and light and the pellets of ice hitting like the sting of bees. Joe sat in the back of the black like a statue taking the hits as they came. Jim might have crouched under the protection of the tarp if it had not been for Rick laying on his back, still in pain and taking up most of the room. The women laughed and carried on joking with each other as the rain came down drenching the men and animals alike. The women were playing a hand of five card draw betting on which man would give up and come into the protection of the wagon first!

  Bobby groaned as Schon shook him awake, he had never felt this bad in his life, "What did I do," he asked as his head exploded in a cascade of light. "I think you drank too much!" Schon answered. Slowly the memory of the night came back to him, "How could I have been so stupid!" he moaned holding his head in his hands. He had to do something to make things right with Michelle. He knew she would not speak to him, Bobby knew she might not even look in his direction. He wanted to tell her she was his world and without her his life would be an empty void, like a desert beast without even so much as a small wind to make their lives tolerable. His head throbbed from the bite of the tequila and his stomach felt as if it had been kicked by an angry bull but it was his heart that hurt the most! "Can I borrow a pencil and paper," Bobby asked quietly, he wanted to write Michelle the greatest love letter anyone had ever written but Bobby was a simple honest man and as he took the pen in hand and wrote his letter to the best of his ability. "I love you, I'm sorry, please forgive me," was all the paper said. Bobby gently folded the paper and handed it to Schon, "Will you see Michelle gets this?" he said. Schon was the same kind of man, "I'll see she gets it!" Schon said as he placed the letter in his own pocket, he knew Bobby's hopes and dreams lay in the small piece of paper and this made it important to them both! Bobby's misery reached into his very soul as he saddled his horse and headed to the Lazy 'B' ranch. Bobby watched as dark clouds formed in the northern sky, today was going to be a day filled with grief and misery. Before he reached the safety of the ranch he was going to be facing the fury of the storm. Mike and Roy both were waiting for Bobby to get home, they were fed up because Bobby was spending all of his time chasing the girl of his dreams. He was on third owner of the Lazy 'B' and that meant on third of the work was his to be done. There was a well to be dug, fences to mend and cattle to brand. Bobby was going to do his share of the work or they were going to give him what for! Even as the storm struck they watched for him out of the window, this was not going to be a happy reunion. Bobby donned his slicker and pulled his hat down facing the down pour. He felt like this was the first day in a life of misery. The rain was coming down in sheets as Bobby rode into the barn; life had kicked him down one too many times. It was out of instinct that he stripped the saddle off the horse and gave the pinto a bucket of grain and it was this same instinct that led him to take a burlap sack and dry the animal before going into the house. Bobby did not want to face the men he called partner and friend until he had a hold of his emotions because he didn't want to break down in front of the men he respected.

Roy and Mike watched as Bobby walked towards the home they shared, it was hard to believe what they saw, Bobby looked like an old man, he was young and strong and vital but he walked with his shoulders pulled in, head down and back hunched staring at his feet as he walked. This was not the Bobby they knew, this Bobby had been broken and whipped by the world around him. The men of the Lazy 'B' worked hard they fought hard and they drank hard but they never stabbed a man in the back or kicked a man while he was down. If they had plans to chew Bobby out they were forgotten now, they knew this man well enough to know just by his action that something was very wrong! Mike poured a cup of coffee and handed it to Bobby as he entered the house hoping the hot liquids would help revive the man's spirits. The rain would keep them in the house for a few more hours which gave them enough time to try to find out what was wrong. Finally Bobby explained to them what had happened between him and Michelle and that Jim was planning a round up and needed their help.

Even as they spoke, the men on the MacCland ranch were planning their own round up. With no owner on the ranch, no wages coming in and no whisky left in the cabinet there was no reason to stay but they were not planning on leaving empty handed. Doug was sullen and quiet as he led the small group of Malloy hands up to the house of the MacCland ranch, they had discussed stealing whatever they could and rustling cattle, this would make them a band of outlaws but who would mess with them? The men at the MacCland ranch were just like them without work or wages, they would listen to them. Skip MacCland had not hired cowboys like the Malloy ranch he hired gunmen and thugs bent on taking over the valley, they were not loyal to the brand, they were there for the money.

Doug didn't care about any of this, his face was disfigured, and the cheap whisky he drank felt like liquid fire as it passed by the stitches in his mouth. His jaw was wired shut and he could not eat or sleep he could not even speak without bolts of pain shooting through his head. Doug was a cruel and vicious man who cared little if at all for human life, he lived on hate and anger. He was a man the others feared and hated, this was the life he chose and enjoyed. He had never been treated like this before and the man responsible for it had to pay and in his eyes the ex-marshal had to pay with his life! As the men rode up to the ranch Doug was already making plans of his won. Daryl sat in the veranda watching as the group of men approached, the last of a bottle of tequila sat beside him, Daryl picked up the bottle and downed the last few drops as they dismounted he didn't have to be told what they wanted, Daryl was not a stupid man he knew what they had been thinking even before they showed up because it was the same thing he was thinking! Doug had been the foreman at the Malloy ranch and because of his raw strength and short temper, at five nine and two hundred pounds of muscle few would dare to oppose the man. Daryl was just the opposite, tall and lanky with a gunfighters build. Daryl used his brains instead of his fists, he was sneaky and smart. Together with the men of both ranches under them they could make a force few if any in the valley could with stand. They would not have to hunt in the brush and draws to gather cattle; they could take what they wanted because cattle out in the open is quick and easy pickings. It didn't matter if they were from the Malloy ranch, the Rocking 'R' or the Lazy 'B', with a dozen men under his control they would not take a hundred head of cattle they would take a thousand! Even with his disfigured face and busted jaw Doug was more of a match for the men that were left, Doug would be his second in command and they would be the largest and strongest gang in ht area, maybe the state!

Doug was not interested in the cattle or Daryl's plans, the only thing he wanted was weapons, and his pistol and rifle were missing, stolen by the same man that had busted his jaw and ran him and his men off the Malloy ranch! While Daryl spoke of friendship and power, Doug searched the house looking for weapons he so desperately wanted. It was in the drawer of Skip's desk that he found the pistol, it was not as nice as the one that was taken from him but it was a forty-four and the shells in his belt were forty-fours. He checked the chamber to make sure the pistol was loaded then slid the revolver into his holster. The fifty caliber Sharps rifle hung over the fire place mantle, he took it down and checked the loads but the rifle was empty so he tore the desk apart looking for shells. Daryl watched as the mad man ripped the place apart looking for the shells. He was not sure if he could trust the man or not but he needed him and now was no time cross him, he do that later after he got what he wanted! "You'll find some fifty caliber shells in the bunk house," Daryl said, hoping to bring the man to his senses. "If you go after the marshal you will have to face the gunfighter and you won't live long when that happens!" Daryl warned. "You think I'm scared of him, Doug asked, with the fifty in my hands I'll kill the both of them before they can get within a hundred yards of me!" Doug was going insane and Daryl was smart enough to know it. "Maybe it wouldn't be so bad with just eleven men under him and besides Doug might get lucky and kill both of them, he said to himself, and even if he died it would leave the valley wide open and he was sure to kill at least one of them before Doug was killed. Daryl knew that if the ex-marshal or the gunman had to crawl, one or both of the men would put a bullet in the ex-foreman of the Malloy ranch!" Daryl threw his hands in the air, "fine, go after them, he said, but we can't help you!" The look of a man possessed was on Doug's face as he turned to face 'Daryl, "just you don't try an stop me, he said as he laid his hand on the butt of the pistol. Daryl knew he was quicker than Doug, he could put three bullets in the man before he cleared leather and in his enraged state of mind Doug might be able to get a shot off even with three slugs in him and Daryl didn't want to wind up gut shot with a dead man at his feet, he was not prepared to take that kind of chance! "Forget it, he said, besides there was no reason to kill the man, he was of importance alive and worth nothing dead and just maybe he could kill the only men that might be capable of stopping them!

Doug went into the bunkhouse where he found a full box of fifty caliber shells sitting in the window sill. He picked up the box, loaded the rifle then put the rest of the shells in his shirt pocket. As he left the bunk house a new gang had formed, maybe the largest gang in the country, and they were all sitting on the front porch watching as dark clouds rolled in from the north. Large drops of water struck the ground kicking up small puffs of dust as Doug put his feet into the stirrups and swung up into the saddle. Daryl watched as the man ride off into the storm and he knew in his heart that this would be the last time he would ever see the man alive, he knew Doug had gone insane!

Doug was not headed for the Malloy ranch he was headed into town, this was going to be a man hunt and he needed supplies. Maybe the doctor would give him some Laudanum for the pain in his jaw, if not then he wanted whisky or tequila, anything to relieve the pain. After that he would need food and once the killing was done he was going to leave the valley for good. If he never saw this place again it would be too soon! In his present state of mind he didn't care if the rain had turned to large chunks of ice and that it was pounding the horse he rode on or that he rode in puddles that rose above the horse's hooves. He didn't care that the creek was half full and rising as he whipped the horse into the raging waters, not until the horse was being swept down river did he realize the danger he was in. Doug tried to free his feet from the stirrups as the horse rolled in the currents. All of a sudden he was remembering that as a child his mother took him to church and the reverend was one of this fire and brimstone preacher who said that Jesus saved those who had taken Christ as their Savior and they would spend eternity walking on streets of gold while the cursed and dammed would spend eternity in a lake of fire to burn forever. Doug wondered if hell would be as bad as a blistering Montana winter as the horse rolled and slammed him into a rock, the weight of the animal broke his back and crushed his ribs as he went under for the last time. The weight on the end of the stirrup acted like a rudder banging at the horse's ribs and legs, spinning it in circles and catching on rocks while brush was pulling it under, then letting go only to grab again as the horse fought for its life, kicking at the ground below desperately trying to reach one bank or another. As the creek widened out the water became shallower and the horse managed to stand. Boiling water of sand and mud rushed under its belly as it started for the bank. Doug's foot slid out of his boot and the weight dragging the horse down was released. It stood on the bank fighting for air as Doug's body was being washed downstream!

The midday sun had turned dark almost to the point of pitch blackness as the storm clouds covered the sky. Thunder vibrated the ground as lightning flashed across the heavens setting fires to the trees and brush below. Hail struck like falling bullets around the home of the Lazy 'B' ranch as Roy and the others stood on the porch watching for the sign of a tornado between the flashes of lightning. Cattle on the open range would have to find shelter for themselves and the horses were already in the barn yet nothing could protect them from the full force of a tornado but the roof of the barn could protect them from the chunks of hail falling from the sky above. As lightning lit up the darkness the outline of a horse could be seen in the distance. Bobby let loose with a shrieking whistle hoping to call the horse in. Chunks of ice the size of a silver dollar pounded the sides of the house unmercifully and if the chunks got any bigger the horse would be beaten to death standing in the open with no place to go! Bobby whistled again as the horse drew nearer. Bobby made a dash for the reins as the horse made its way into the yard. Hail struck like balled fists trying to knock the man unconscious as he mounted the horse and ride for the barn. Bobby lit a lantern then took the saddle off the shivering animal. Long cuts ran down the sides and chest where patches of hair were torn from its hide. Even in this light Bobby suspected what had happened, someone had tried to cross a creek that had turned into a river and had sucked rider and horse alike downstream and this was the result, a horse in torment and somewhere out there was a man afoot or dead. In a storm like this the odds of survival were not good. Bobby knew the rider was most likely dead and to go out looking for the man or woman now was to put more lives at risk. Later after the storm they would go out looking for the body, but for now he would take care of the injured animal. Bobby placed oats in the trough in a stall then led the horse in, then taking a burlap sack he began to wipe the water from the freezing animal and then put liniment on the wounds, later after the storm one of them would go for the vet.

Bobby listened to the hail pound on the roof of the barn as he waited for the chunks of ice to turn into rain before heading back to the house. The others would be waiting for him on the porch. This time they would not be riding to help Jim on a round up, they would be going to find a missing rider. The body would probably be washed downstream by the raging water of a flash flood.

The Old Rider

The storm was passing as Mike and Roy ran for the barn. Dry Texas ground had turned to mud sticking to their boots as they ran. Both men knew they were on a mission of mercy, the rider in the storm might still be alive yet even as they saddled their horses they knew the odds of survival were slim but there was still a chance and every second counted. The injured horse was now on its own, they had to find the rider first. They would back track the animal as far as they could, following the hoof prints as far as they could up to the point where the rain washed them away then they would have to guess which direction to take to find the missing rider. Doug lay half submerged in the receding water as Roy and Mike approached. Sand and mud was packed into the mouth and nostrils of the drowned man and was washed out of the lungs as they drug him from the creek, washing away the filth. "We'll bury him on top of the hill," Roy said placing a rope around the man's chest and using his horse to drag the corpse up the steep grade. As the men dug the shallow grave they could not help but think one day this was going to be a great place to live, a place to be proud of, a place where men could raise cattle and families alike but until the killing stopped it was a no man's land fit only for the wild animals that roamed the valley.